JERNIGAN

After a week-long spending spree in El Paso following the sale of the broncos he's spent six months catching, Ed Jernigan boards a stagecoach back to Rincon. On the journey, he meets the beautiful Margaret Leland, owner of the Crescent Ranch. He hardly has the chance to get to know her, however, before a gang of outlaws holds up the stage and leaves an elderly passenger dead. Swearing revenge, Jernigan tracks the thieves down and retrieves the loot. Arriving in Rincon and checking in to a hotel, he's surprised to find Margaret there and returns her possessions — and is rewarded with the unexpected offer of a job as range detective at her ranch. Her stepson and his shady friends are causing trouble, and might have had a hand in her late husband's death. Is Jernigan up to the task?

SPECIAL MESSAGE TO READERS

THE ULVERSCROFT FOUNDATION
(registered UK charity number 264873)
was established in 1972 to provide funds for
research, diagnosis and treatment of eye diseases.
Examples of major projects funded by
the Ulverscroft Foundation are:-

- The Children's Eye Unit at Moorfields Eye Hospital, London
- The Ulverscroft Children's Eye Unit at Great Ormond Street Hospital for Sick Children
- Funding research into eye diseases and treatment at the Department of Ophthalmology, University of Leicester
- The Ulverscroft Vision Research Group, Institute of Child Health
- Twin operating theatres at the Western Ophthalmic Hospital, London
- The Chair of Ophthalmology at the Royal Australian College of Ophthalmologists

You can help further the work of the Foundation
by making a donation or leaving a legacy.
Every contribution is gratefully received. If you
would like to help support the Foundation or
require further information, please contact:

THE ULVERSCROFT FOUNDATION
The Green, Bradgate Road, Anstey
Leicester LE7 7FU, England
Tel: (0116) 236 4325

website: www.foundation.ulverscroft.com

JERNIGAN

JOHN CALLAHAN

SAGEBRUSH
Large Print Westerns

First published in the United States by Ace Books

First Isis Edition
published 2019
by arrangement with
Golden West Literary Agency

A catalogue record for this book is available
from the British Library.

ISBN 978–1–78541–564–7 (pb)

Published by
F. A. Thorpe (Publishing)
Anstey, Leicestershire

Set by Words & Graphics Ltd.
Anstey, Leicestershire
Printed and bound in Great Britain by
T. J. International Ltd., Padstow, Cornwall

This book is printed on acid-free paper

When leaving the train at Lordsburg, to take the stage north to Rincon, Ed Jernigan was not yet over the hangover of his week-long spree in El Paso. His head still ached, and the motion of the cars had done nothing to ease the queasiness in his stomach. He was also in a foul temper, for too much of his hard-earned money had found its way over the bars, across the gambling tables, and into the silken stockings of Paso's gay ladies.

Hard-earned money it had indeed been, for Jernigan mustanged back in the Brenoso Badlands — and if there was a harder way to earn a dollar than catching and breaking wild horses, he'd never heard of it.

Still, he was the man for such work. He had a strong back, and, he claimed, a weak mind. Actually, he was a big man and a tough one. A transplanted Texan now, having settled in the Territory of New Mexico, he had grown up on the Texas frontier when the Comanches still raided and the outlaws prowled. At fourteen he'd been left a range orphan, thanks to the fever that took his mother and the horse thief that killed his father. He had survived on his own, for sixteen long, hard years now, and that meant his toughness was as much mental as physical. The truth was, Ed Jernigan possessed the craftiness of all creatures who managed to stay alive in a savage land.

He had just enough time for one stiff drink to perk him up somewhat, but he was still not wholly himself when arriving at the waiting stagecoach.

The other passengers were having the driver stow their luggage away in the rear boot, but he held on to his valise. He wanted to keep it with him because it held, along with his range clothes, his razor and his gunrig, what was left of his horse money: a bit more than a thousand dollars. He'd squandered about six hundred during his week in El Paso. *Easy come, easy go. Ha*, he thought.

The stage had three other passengers. A city man, of beefy body and ruddy face, who was probably a drummer. A scrawny, weather-beaten old-timer who looked like a raggedy-pants rancher. A young woman with a face and figure right out of a bachelor's dreams. Jernigan looked at her, then looked again and almost forgot he was suffering from a hangover. She was something of a beauty ... Auburn-haired, with amber-flecked brown eyes and a creamy complexion. Wearing a dark-green traveling outfit that looked costly enough to make her a rich man's wife or daughter.

The driver, a whiskery old man, said peevishly, "Well, get aboard, the lot of you. We'll be rolling directly I get this tied down."

He was already tying down the boot's leather apron.

The coach door stood open, and the young woman made for it.

2

Jernigan hastened to offer her a hand. "Allow me, ma'am," he said, putting that hand to her left elbow.

She rather needed it, for she had to gather her long, full skirt up with one hand to raise a small foot to the step while holding her reticule in the other. With his help she rose easily and gracefully, and then inside and seated, she smiled out at him.

"Thank you."

"My pleasure, ma'am."

Jernigan hadn't quite forgotten his hangover because of her, and now hesitated to ride inside where it would be stuffy and dusty. He needed air, and plenty of it.

Looking at the driver, he said, "Ride with you on the box?"

"Not likely," the oldster said. "I'm carrying a shotgun messenger."

At that moment that worthy came from the stage company's office. He carried not a shotgun but an ancient Henry rifle. He was a dour-looking man with a shaggy sorrel moustache. He moved with a lazy shuffle, and at that moment stifled a yawn. He didn't inspire confidence, but then, Jernigan reminded himself, the Apaches were corraled on their reservations and seldom went bronco any more, while the white renegades didn't hit every stagecoach.

With that thought, he followed the drummer and the raggedy-pants cowman aboard. Pulling the door shut behind him, he seated himself opposite the young woman passenger. She met his gaze and smiled faintly, acknowledging that his small courtesy toward her made him a gentleman in her eyes.

3

Despite his headachy, queasy feeling and his bad humor, Jernigan smiled back. He had a sort of charm when he smiled, and he was handsome in a rough-hewn way. He'd shaved that morning, and he'd had his faded yellow hair cut only days ago. He was wearing what he called his Sunday clothes: his good Stetson, light gray in color and flat-crowned, his dark-gray broadcloth suit, a white shirt with a maroon string tie, his black hand-tooled boots. Covertly, the young woman took in his appearance. This, despite the fact that she was a married woman. At least, there showed through a brown kid glove the outline of a ring on the third finger of her left hand — and Jernigan took it to be a wedding band.

"Going far, ma'am?"

"Only so far as Rincon, by this stagecoach."

"Come from El Paso?"

"Yes. I've been visiting my sister there. She lives at Fort Bliss. Her husband is an Army officer. And you?"

"Drove some horses to Paso," he told her. "Sold them and then saw the elephant. Er, the sights, I mean, ma'am. Going to Rincon, too. Then home to the Brenoso. Name's Ed Jernigan."

"Mine is Margaret Leland."

"Missus?"

"Well, yes," said Margaret Leland.

The grizzled old driver and his lazy-looking gun guard had climbed to the box, and now with a wild yell and a pistol-shot crack of the whip the six-horse team was turned loose. The Concord coach gave a great lurch, swayed wildly on its thoroughbraces, and the

4

adobe buildings and houses of Lordsburg began to fall behind. The driver kept his animals running hard for a spell, and the dun-colored dust roiled up from under pounding hooves and spinning wheels.

The sun laid its heavy heat all about, and the interior of the coach became as stuffy as Jernigan had anticipated. He pushed his hat back from his brow, unknotted his tie, unbuttoned his shirt collar, removed his coat and laid it on his lap. The drummer fanned himself with his narrow-brimmed hat, and his pudgy face kept getting redder and redder. The old cowman dozed with his bony chin on his chest, unaffected by heat, dust or bumpy, swaying motion. Mrs. Leland removed her gloves, then her saucy little hat. Finally she took an embroidered handkerchief from her reticule and coughed daintily into it.

Jernigan saw that she did indeed wear a wedding ring. It was a quarter-inch band of gold, big enough to warn a man off at twenty paces. Mr. Leland hadn't done any skimping when he took her into double harness. He would have had to brand her to make it more obvious that she was private property.

Jernigan decided he didn't blame the man. But if he'd been in Mr. Leland's boots he wouldn't have let her go sashaying off to El Paso or anywhere else alone. He would have kept her handy, a woman like that. Mr. Leland must be, Jernigan reflected, one of those men who have all the luck in this world.

Me, that's what I need . . . A woman to do my cooking and warm my bed — and to keep me from helling around when I get a little money.

The thought startled Jernigan, being one he'd never before entertained. But it was a valid idea, worthy of some consideration. After all, he was thirty years old — and felt ninety. Time he was settled down with a wife and a couple of kids. Strange, his not having realized that before now.

Trouble was, a man didn't have a lot of choice. The Territory wasn't so settled up that a man could look around and decide which woman would do for him. What few marriageable women happened along were gobbled up in a hurry.

Besides, what woman would want to live on the edge of the badlands, as he did, and not see a face other than her husband's from one month to another? What woman would be willing to live in an adobe hut with furniture knocked together out of planks with a hammer and a saw? What woman would want to be married to a mustanger, a loco thing for a man to be?

Could find me a cute little Mexican girl . . . Take her to her padre and have him tie the knot.

Trouble with *that* was, he'd have to spend the rest of his life eating tacos and frijoles and everything else fiery with chili — and Mexican cooking gave him heartburn.

Forget it, Ed . . . You're just envying Mr. Leland his luck. The only way you'll ever have a wife like his is in your dreams.

Mr. Leland's wife again coughed daintily into her handkerchief.

Jernigan said to her, "Smoke and cinders on the train, dust on a stage. These modern ways of traveling sure aren't all they're cracked up to be."

6

"How right you are, Mr. Jernigan," Mrs. Leland said, smiling at him now that her coughing had subsided.

Real friendly, he thought. Almost a flirty smile. He wondered about Mr. Leland.

"Horses, they're my business," he ventured. "What does Mr. Leland do?"

"Mr. Leland . . . ?" She seemed to have forgotten there was such a person. "Oh, he's in the cattle business. He owns a rather large ranch. Crescent Ranch. You've heard of it?"

"Yes, ma'am," Jernigan said. "I've heard of Crescent Ranch, all right."

And indeed he had. Everybody had heard of that outfit. Everybody in this part of the Territory, anyway. A big, greedy outfit. Grabbing up range all over creation. Squeezing the little ranchers out. Using hired gunhands to do it. The piece of range Crescent had gobbled up most recently lay just beyond the Hondo Hills from the *malpais* where he, Ed Jernigan, did his mustanging. A good thing the Brenoso Badlands wasn't fit for cattle, else Mr. Leland might decide to push him out. A nice lady, Mrs. Leland. But Mr. Leland . . .

I'd shoot him sure if he tried to steal range from me . . . I'd slip past his gunhands and do him in, for certain.

"Something wrong, Mr. Jernigan?"

"Wrong, ma'am?"

"You were scowling so — so ferociously."

"Had a bad thought," he said, a bit shamefacedly.

They made a scheduled stop at the Peso Creek stage station for a change of horses, and then, a couple of miles farther on, an unscheduled one. This was rough country, all brush and rocks, and the fresh team was taking it slow and easy up a long grade when a rifle shot cracked. That was when the rig made its second stop.

Margaret Leland looked alarmed, and gasped, "What's happened?"

The drummer, looking scared, muttered, "A holdup sure!"

The old cowman woke up but didn't say anything, didn't even look concerned.

Jernigan also took it to be a holdup attempt. He stuck his head out the window and saw that the team's off leader was down, dead in its tracks. He also saw three riders emerge from a jumble of huge rocks. They wore neckscarves over the lower half of their faces. They had their guns aimed at the stagecoach. The driver was cursing bitterly, but the shotgun messenger was as quiet as a mouse.

"We ain't carrying no strongbox, you no-good sons."

That from the driver.

"Easy, boys; I've got my hands up."

That from the gun guard.

"If you're carrying no express, we'll have to take up a collection," one of the road agents said, talking loud so he could be heard through his red bandanna mask. "Everybody down and line up. We're going to pass the hat. All donations gratefully accepted, and all contributions for a good cause. Hurry it up, folks!"

Jernigan swore under his breath, thinking of his six-shooter shut up in his valise there between him and the drummer on the seat. No chance to get it out. Better not, anyway. Shooting, and the lady might get hit. He also thought of his thousand dollars in gold and silver specie, it too in the valise. Maybe the holdup trio wouldn't look into the coach. He hoped. He opened the door and climbed out, then turned to help Margaret Leland down. He marveled at her calm. No hysterical female, she. She gave him a brave little smile.

Soon they were all lined up beside the coach, facing the three masked, mounted men and their cocked, leveled guns.

"You, *muchacho* . . . Get down and take their money and valuables."

The man giving that order was the one who had spoken before. He was big and burly, and like his partners, wearing shabby garb. Their seedy appearance suggested that the road agent business wasn't too good. The one who dismounted, *el muchacho*, was small and wiry. Mexican certainly, with his dusky skin, brown eyes and black hair. The third man of average build. He seemed young, and he was definitely edgy. His gun kept moving to and fro, its muzzle first on one victim and then on another.

Jernigan looked from him to the burly man. "Your young friend, there . . . Tell him to point that gun elsewhere. Jumpy as he is, it could go off any second — and it could be the lady he shoots."

The burly man said, "Yeah, Chuck; be careful. Ease your hammer down. We're not going to have any trouble with this bunch. They're all nice folks."

Chuck muttered a protest, but did as he was told. With that one's gun no longer cocked, Jernigan breathed easier. He was still worried about his valise, however. He hoped the *muchacho* wouldn't look into the coach and spot it.

The Mexican pulled an empty flour sack from his pocket. With his gun still in his right hand, he held the sack open as he went to the angry stage driver. Both the driver and the gun guard dropped what money they carried into the sack. The drummer was next, and he grudgingly added his wallet and some change to the pot.

"Your watch too, dude," the burly man said. "Pronto!"

The drummer's watch and chain also went grudgingly into the sack.

The Mexican came next to the old cowman. When that one dropped only a couple of silver dollars and a few smaller coins in, the Mexican became infuriated at such slim pickings. Cursing in Spanish, he brought his gun up and slammed the barrel hard against the old-timer's jaw. The cowman fell back against the coach, hung there limply for a moment, then crumpled to the ground and lay sprawled face-down.

Jernigan swore under his breath, and Margaret Leland, gazing angrily at the little bandit, said, "That wasn't necessary. What are you, a savage?"

The Mexican turned to her, again raising his gun like a club. His dark eyes were mean above his mask, and he cursed her as he had the old cowman.

Jernigan burst out, "Hombre, you hit her you'd better kill me — because I'll sure as shooting hunt you down and kill you!"

Now the Mexican stared at him, but after a moment he lowered his gun and again held the sack with both hands.

To Margaret, he said, "Get your money out, *gringa!*"

She took her purse from her reticule and added it to the collection. He saw her wedding ring.

"That too," he said, snarling the words. "Take it off!"

Jernigan again spoke to the burly man. "Let her keep it. It has meaning for her, and wouldn't be worth much to you."

The burly man said, "Friend, you talk too much."

Margaret said, "Please, Mr. Jernigan — never mind." She twisted the ring from her finger and dropped it into the sack.

Now it was Jernigan's turn, and he emptied his pockets. A couple of goldpieces, a single crumpled banknote, some silver dollars, a small handful of pennies and other coins. As he dropped the money into the sack, the Mexican looked at him with mocking eyes.

"*Gracias, gringo . . . Muchas gracias.*"

He started to back away, toward his horse.

The burly man said, "Wait a minute, *muchacho* . . . . Look in the coach. Sometimes they leave money and valuables inside when a stage gets jumped."

Jernigan swore again under his breath. What he said would have shocked a muleskinner, and Margaret Leland caught some of it. She gave him a startled look.

The Mexican saw the valise, of course. He hauled it out, dropped it and his sack of loot to the ground. Holstering his gun, he knelt by the valise and unbuckled its straps. He rummaged in the valise, once

11

it was open. He threw out Jernigan's old hat and boots, his gunrig, then let loose with a gleeful yelp as he came up with the leather pouch containing the horse money. By now Jernigan was thinking he should have stayed longer in El Paso and let the bartenders, gamblers and fancy ladies take all that money. A man was robbed that way too but it was more fun than being robbed this way.

The Mexican gave the pouch a shake, and there was a musical jingle of gold and silver coins.

"Plenty of money here, *por Dios!*"

"Fetch it," the burly man said, sounding as happy as the *muchacho*. "Come along with it. Let's get out of here before somebody happens along!"

The Mexican dropped Jernigan's pouch into the sack, carried the sack to the burly man. The latter hefted it, then, with a chuckle, thrust it into one of his saddlebags.

"Nice pickings," he said. "We're obliged to you folks." He gestured with his gun. "Now walk down the road a piece. Come on — move!"

The stage driver and his gun guard started away, and the drummer followed them. Taking Margaret Leland's arm, Jernigan led her after the three. He glanced down at the old cowman, who hadn't moved since falling, and wondered if he was dead, unconscious or just playing possum.

Margaret said, "Why are they making us walk, Mr. Jernigan?"

"They're not bothering to take the guns the driver and the guard and I left behind," he said. "They're not

12

giving us a chance to grab and use them when they ride out."

"That one . . . hitting that poor old man. Did you lose much money?"

"What I had left from selling forty-three broncs," he said sourly. "The six months of catching and breaking them gone. How about you?"

"A little more than forty dollars."

"I'll try to get it back for you."

She gave him a wide-eyed look, started to say something. Before she could speak, there was a yell from the burly man.

"Come on, come on! Let's head for the tules!"

The three were in motion then, but immediately there was another yell.

"No, you don't, you sneaky old galoot!"

And a gun blasted.

Jernigan swung about, at the same time pushing the woman behind him. He saw that the old cowman had been merely playing possum. Coming alive as the bandits started away, the old-timer had grabbed up Jernigan's gun and fired a shot at the three. It had gone wild. Now, having risen to his knees and one hand, he was aiming for a second shot. Two of the bandits, the burly man and the Mexican, kept on going — spurring their horses to a hard run. The third, the young, edgy one, had pulled up and swung his mount about and was now drawing a bead on the cowman.

A shout rose in Jernigan's throat, but he choked it back. Nothing could stop this. Nothing did, and when it happened, with the bandit's gun roaring once, twice and a third time, Jernigan flinched as though the slugs were coming his way instead of slamming into the old man's gaunted body.

The youthful bandit lifted his gaze. Seeing Jernigan watching him, he raised his still smoking gun as though to add another notch to it. His neckscarf mask slipped down from his face, and his mouth was formed in an ugly grin.

"That'll show him!" he yelled. "That'll show the lot of you!"

He reined his horse about and rode at a gallop after the other two.

Jernigan started running toward the bullet-riddled old cowman even before the bandits had lost themselves among the brush and rocks to the west of the stage trail. He had no need to kneel by the loosely sprawled body and feel to make sure there was no heartbeat. The gaping mouth, the vacant, staring eyes, the spilled blood, all told him that the old-timer was dead.

He knew then, if he hadn't before, that he was going after those three — and keeping after them until he got them, no matter how long it took.

II

Jernigan picked up the gun, his gun, that the old-timer had so foolhardily turned on the road agents. He picked up his gunrig too, thrust the revolver into the holster, and buckled the cartridge-studded belt about

14

his waist. He reached into the boot of the stagecoach for the shotgun messenger's ancient Henry rifle.

"This thing," he said, as the gun guard came up with the driver and the drummer. "Is it loaded?"

"Sure is," the gun guard said. "Fifteen rounds. Why ask?"

"I'm taking it with me," Jernigan said. "I'm going after those three."

"Afoot?" the driver said. "You're loco, man. You'd never catch up with them."

"I'll catch up with them," Jerigan said, his voice abrasive with anger. "I'll get me a horse at the stage station. Somebody gather up my gear and take it along to Rincon."

He started away, back along the road toward Peso Creek.

Margaret Leland called after him, "Be careful."

He nodded, and grim-faced, went on.

Half an hour later, riding a borrowed horse, which he had promised the station agent would be turned in at the stage company's Rincon stable, he tracked the three bandits through the rough country stretching to the mountains far to the west. He hadn't a lot of daylight left for his tracking, but just after the sun dropped behind the jagged peaks, he came to a place along a little creek where the trio had had a camp and picked up a spare horse. A pack animal, he supposed. The tracks of the four horses led southeast.

An hour later he topped a rise and saw a pinpoint of light far ahead. He reined in and peered at it, decided after a moment that it was not a ranchhouse light but the flickering glare of a campfire. He rode toward it at a slow walk, then dismounted and tied the dun among some brush at the base of a towering rock. Taking the old Henry rifle with him, he went on afoot.

He came to a deep arroyo and dropped into it. It led him to within twenty yards of the campfire, and there they were — the three of them. The Mexican was cooking up a meal, and the other two were counting the loot. They'd dumped it out of the flour sack onto a spread blanket. At the moment they were gloating over the contents of Jernigan's pouch.

The Mexican looked up from frying bacon. "How much, *amigos?*"

"A thousand dollars," the burly man said. "What a haul!"

Jernigan recognized him, now that his face was uncovered. He'd seen him around Rincon a time or two, a barroom hanger-on. A rough, tough hombre, by name Matt Baylor.

Working the Henry's lever, Jernigan said, "Just stay as you are, you ornery sons. I'll drop the one who moves a hair."

They froze, the *muchacho* bending over the fire and the other two where they sat crosslegged with the loot between them.

"Just who're you, hombre?" Baylor demanded, sounding scared — and offended. "What's the idea, sneaking up on us like a damn Apache?"

"My name's Jernigan, if you've got to know. More important, I'm the owner of that thousand dollars. Put it back in the sack — all of it."

16

For emphasis, he fired a shot. The slug scattered sparks and burning brands from the fire. It tipped over the *muchacho's* skillet. Spilled grease flamed up, made a great glare.

"The next shot," Jernigan said, throwing another cartridege into the Henry's chamber, "will be for you, Baylor. Now get on with it, like I told you."

Baylor swore bitterly, but reached for the sack and held it so the youthful bandit, Chuck, could drop the loot into it. The Mexican had backed off a step, to get away from the burning grease.

"That far and no farther," Jernigan told him, coming out of the arroyo.

He took a few steps toward the camp, decided that was close enough. He was getting the loot back, but somehow felt far from satisfied. That young one, Chuck . . . he'd killed the old-timer and he shouldn't be getting away with it. The three of them shouldn't be getting off scot-free after having pulled the holdup. Take them to Rincon and turn them over to the law? Uh-huh. The law wasn't much in these parts. Besides, he was no hero. Not hero enough to try taking three desperadoes across maybe thirty miles of empty country. They'd find a way to jump him. And once they jumped him, they would surely kill him.

Too bad I'm not a killer . . . I should be judge, jury and executioner — and leave them here for the buzzards.

The blanket was cleaned off, the sack bulging.

Jernigan said, "Now I'll tell you, Baylor . . . You shuck your gun and bring that sack out here to me.

17

Stand up with it, then get rid of your six-shooter. Easy now."

Baylor did some muttered cursing but heaved to his feet with the sack in his left hand. With his right, he unbuckled his gunrig and let it drop to the ground. With laggard step, he moved toward Jernigan. Behind him, Chuck came erect. Jernigan now watched him more closely than Matt Baylor. Some instinct he'd developed during his years of surviving in a hostile land warned him that Chuck was going to make a play.

Had he planned it this way, without being aware that he was?

Was that why he hadn't ordered Chuck and the Mexican to shuck their guns?

Maybe.

Maybe he wanted Chuck to make a play, so he could settle with him for killing the old cowman. Sometimes a man didn't quite know his own mind.

Baylor was now within ten feet of him, close enough.

"Set it down," Jernigan told him. "Set it down and back off."

Baylor obeyed with the expected reluctance of a man letting loose of what was to him a small fortune. He bent, laid the sack on the ground, then straightened and took a couple of backward steps before turning. Jernigan strode forward and was reaching for the sack when Chuck made his play. His fool play, as Jernigan thought it.

Shifting his position to a gunfighter's stance, Chuck yelled, "Watch it, Matt!" Then he grabbed out his gun, and he was fast — very fast. He slammed a shot at

Jernigan even as the mustanger flung himself flat. He got off a second shot as Jernigan brought the Henry to his shoulder. The slug struck so close it kicked dirt into Jernigan's face, causing him to flinch and utter a startled grunt. He was about to squeeze off a third shot when the old Henry spat powder-flame.

If a man had to do some shooting, Jernigan always figured, he should do it with a rifle. With a rifle, you could mostly put a slug where you wanted. A handgun wasn't half so dependable, unless you had it sticking in a man's belly.

His slug caught Chuck where he wanted it to, dead-center in the chest. Chuck staggered under the impact, and his gun fired its third shot into the ground by his own feet. He reeled this way and that for a moment, then toppled forward like a felled tree. He landed face-down, and did not move again. He wasn't going to move ever again, Jernigan knew.

Matt Baylor had thrown himself down when Chuck started his play. Now he was up and running, heading away from the camp to lose himself in the darkness. But the *muchacho* . . . he had drawn his gun and was cutting loose with it.

Another foolish one, Jernigan thought.

The Henry cracked again, and the Mexican let out a yelp. His gun flew from his hand as though he'd thrown it away. He clapped his left hand to his right shoulder, where the Henry's slug had drilled him, and he began to curse bitterly in Spanish.

Jernigan muttered, "So be it," and got to his feet with the rifle in one hand and the sack of loot in the other.

He backed off to the arroyo, dropped into it. They could no longer see him when he bent low behind the gully's high bank. He set out along the arroyo at a run.

Matt Baylor's angry shout followed him. "You, Jernigan, you tricky son . . . You've killed my brother, and I'll get you for it — if it's the last thing I ever do, by damn!"

He kept on cursing until Jernigan was out of earshot.

Jernigan would have to watch himself from now on. Blood ties were strong, and when a man had a brother killed, he was almost certain to want revenge.

He didn't feel at all good about the killing, even though Chuck had asked for it and deserved it. Looking at it in one way, Chuck had been too young to die. Looking at it in another, he would have certainly have done some more killing of his own if he had lived.

A hell of a thing, anyway, Jernigan thought.

He was feeling a little guilty, being aware that he had half-known Chuck would make a play and had deliberately given him the chance to make it.

Reaching his horse, he thrust the sack of loot into one of the saddlebags before untying the reins. He mounted and rode back the way he had come, lifting the animal to an easy lope. He closed his mind to thoughts of what had happened. He wasn't going to let his conscience nag him, damn it.

He rode into Rincon well after midnight, and just about the whole town was asleep. Finding nobody at the stage company stables, he off-saddled the dun and turned it into one of the corrals. With the saddlebags draped over his left shoulder and the Henry rifle in his right hand, he walked along the deserted main street. There were few lights. One was in the lobby of the Territorial House. He reckoned he would take a room there after he'd found something to eat. He was wolf-hungry by now. The town's two eating places were dark, but two of the saloons still spilled yellow lamplight from their windows. He chose the smaller, the Longhorn.

Sam Turnbull, the owner, was dozing on a stool behind the bar. Four townsmen were having a quiet game of poker at a table in the corner. Otherwise, the place was empty.

Turnbull roused, came off the stool, set out a bottle and a glass. He had a moustache and pomaded hair, both rust-red in color.

"Catch up with those holdup men, Jernigan?"

The poker players halted their game to catch Jernigan's reply. He laid his rifle and saddlebags on the bar, poured a drink.

"I caught up with them. The one who killed that old-timer is dead. One of the others has a shoulder he won't use for a spell."

He downed the drink, refilled the glass.

"Why didn't you kill the lot of them, friend?"

That came from one of the poker players. He was a pale shade of a man who peered at the world through spectacles. He looked as though he himself would shrink from killing a fly.

Jernigan said sourly, "Killing's not my business." He downed the second drink. Rotgut whiskey, it took his breath away and felt fiery going down. "Sam, can you rustle me up a little grub?"

The saloonman nodded. "Sure, Ed." He was eyeing the saddlebags. "You brought back what was stolen?"

"That I did," Jernigan said. "The others who were robbed can pick up their money and valuables at the hotel in the morning."

Turnbull rustled up some food from the back room. Cheese, crackers, a flat can of sardines, and a round one of tomatoes. Jernigan wolfed it all down, then had another shot of rotgut to help it digest while he slept. He asked Turnbull what he owed.

"On the house, Ed," the saloonkeeper said. "You've earned a bait of grub and a few drinks. You did what the law around here couldn't or wouldn't have done. By damn, you should be wearing Mel Harper's badge."

Jernigan shook his head to that, and leaving the Longhorn, with his saddlebags and rifle, he told himself he would rather hunt mustangs than outlaws. Wild horses could wear a man down to a frazzle but they couldn't do any shooting.

At the Territorial House, he banged the bell on the counter in the lobby. The proprietor, Hiram Walther, a hugely fat man, came from his room behind the counter in carpet slippers and stuffed his nightshirt into his pants from which the suspenders dangled.

"Oh, it's you, Jernigan," Walther said, focusing his sleepy eyes. "Heard you went after the hombres who held up the stage."

"I went and I'm back and I want a room."

22

Signing the register, he saw the name *Mrs. M. Leland* in neat script just above his scrawl.

"Mrs. Leland . . . she's here?"

The hotelman nodded ponderously. "She decided to stay overnight on the chance that you'd come in with the money and ring she lost."

"Tell her in the morning that I've got them."

Heading for the stairs, he looked at the number of the tag attached to the key Walther had given him. Room Twelve.

He let himself in, locked the door, struck a match, lit the oil lamp. He took the loot sack from the saddlebags and dumped its contents onto the bed. After separating his money from the belongings of the others, he gratefully crawled into bed.

He realized that his week of painting El Paso a bright shade of red had taken more out of him than a week of mustanging would have done.

Getting too old for sowing wild oats . . . Should have me a wife to settle down with.

He fell asleep with that thought, slept like a log, and overslept. The room was filled with bright sunlight when he awoke, and street sounds told him that everybody else was already up and about trying to earn a dollar. He was lying there thinking about rising and shining, himself, when somebody knocked on the door.

"Who's there?"

"The chambermaid, sir. I have your bag. The express office sent it over."

"Put it down there," he called back. "And if you've got time fetch me some hot water."

"Yes, sir."

After the maid returned with the warm water, he washed up, then decided to shave. It wasn't like him to shave two mornings in a row, and he supposed he was doing so now in anticipation of seeing Mr. Leland's beauteous wife again. Realizing that, he made a mocking face at his reflection in the foggy, speckled mirror.

He was lathered up and scraping away with his razor when another knock sounded.

Going on with his shaving, he called, "The door's unlocked. Come on in."

The person who entered shut the door, stood by it, didn't say anything.

"Be with you in a minute," Jernigan said, then saw who it was by way of the mirror.

Mrs. Leland.

He thought: *Well, I'll be durned*. He was bare from the belt up, and suddenly conscious of it. Then he decided: *Well, she's a married woman and knows what the male animal is like.*

As he he kept working with his razor, Margaret said, "I was concerned, Mr. Jernigan. I didn't sleep too well."

"Oh, I got your money and ring back," he said. "They're in those saddlebags. Help yourself."

She didn't move. "I was concerned about you, not about my money and ring."

That brought him around, to stare at her. "About me, ma'am?"

24

As he stared, he thought: *Man, what a lovely creature . . . Prettier than a paint pony.*

"You shouldn't have taken such a risk. They might have killed you."

He'd not had anybody show concern about him in sixteen years, not since he lost his parents. He didn't know how to take it.

"It wasn't likely," he said. "They were boot tough and wolf mean, but all three together didn't have the sense of a jughead mule."

"Did you have to fight them?"

"Well, just a little."

Her eyes widened. "What does that mean?"

"I had to do some shooting. The one who killed the old man got himself killed, and the Mexican took a bullet in the shoulder."

She let her gaze drop from his face to his bare shoulders and chest. She took in the assorted scars of past wounds and injuries that marked his hide with much of his history.

She looked at his face again. "I can see I needn't have worried. You can take care of yourself in any sort of trouble."

"I always have, ma'am."

He laid his razor down, wiped his face clean of lather with a towel, then got her ring, money and purse from the loot sack.

She accepted them with a thank-you, and he noticed that she placed the ring as well as the money in the purse. That made him wonder.

"Well," she said, "since you are all right . . . ."

But she didn't go. She stood there looking at him in a speculative way. He was beginning to think she better had go.

"Mr. Leland . . . he didn't come to meet you?"

"No, he didn't," she said. Then, still looking at him in that thoughtful way: "Could we have a talk later, Mr. Jernigan? If you're going to breakfast, I could meet you then."

He nodded, and then, as she went out, he wondered what a woman like her would have to talk about with a man like him. And where, come to think of it, was Mr. Leland that he hadn't been on hand to meet her after she'd been off visiting in El Paso?

Turning back to the mirror to finish his shaving, Jernigan told his reflection: *Watch your step, bucko . . . Just being suspected of rustling another man's wife could get you in more trouble than if you ran off all his cattle.*

III

She was waiting in the lobby. So was the drummer. Jernigan had the saddlebags along, and the Henry rifle too. He gave the drummer his watch and chain and his money. Pleased, the drummer said, "Friend, I feel that I should reward you."

"Buy me a drink later," Jernigan told him.

He started out with Margaret Leland, telling her, "I'll drop this rifle and the rest of the loot off at the stage company office."

26

She said, "Yes." She was watching him closely, sizing him up, speculating about him. She was making him feel edgy.

Outside, right in front of the hotel, stood a topless, double-hitched buggy. A fancy rig, the body a shiny black and the wheels a bright yellow. A pair of matched grays in gleaming harness. The horses bore the Crescent brand, a quarter-moon. Margaret's luggage was tied on behind. A sombreroed Mexican sat in the rig, holding the reins, a study in patience.

"I won't be long now, Pedro," Margaret said.

"*Sí, señora.*"

Jernigan thought about that. Mr. Leland hadn't come, but he had sent the rig for her.

He dropped the saddlebags and rifle off at the stage company office, explaining to the agent that except for a couple of dollars that had belonged to the old cowman, the money in the loot sack had been taken from the stagedriver and his shotgun messenger.

With Margaret, he walked to the Welcome Café. She was a rather tall young woman, the top of her head a bit higher than his shoulder. Her red-brown hair had a burnished brightness in the sunlight. She was wearing a brown silk dress a bit too stylish and elegant for the dusty street of a grubby town like Rincon. A couple of passing townswomen, in calico and sunbonnets, gave her wide-eyed looks of mingled envy and resentment. The men who passed were covertly admiring.

Three riders came loping into town from the west and pulled up in front of the Alhambra Saloon on the opposite side of the street. Before dismounting they stared across at Jernigan and his companion.

"Early in the day for men to ride in for a drink," he said. He could see the quarter-moon brand on their mounts. "Crescent hands, eh?"

"Brad must have sent them to find out why Pedro didn't get me home last night."

"Brad?" Jernigan said, following her into the restaurant.

"Brad Leland," she said over her shoulder.

The breakfast hour was long past, and the restaurant therefore empty. They seated themselves at a table.

Jernigan said, "I'd have thought Mr. Leland would be concerned enough to come himself."

"Oh, he wouldn't be all that worried about me."

"He wouldn't?"

Before she could reply to that, the waitress came. He ordered ham and eggs, fried potatoes, coffee. Margaret said she would have only coffee.

When they were alone again, she looked at Jernigan a bit shamefacedly. "I'm afraid I've given you the wrong impression, Mr. Jernigan. I've been saying there is a Mr. Leland, which there is. But he's not my husband. I wear my wedding ring when I travel because it discourages men from making overtures I wouldn't welcome. Actually, I'm a widow and the only Mr. Leland now is my brother-in-law, Brad. And he happens to have a wife."

Jernigan said, "A widow." He felt as shaken up as he always did after a first attempt at saddle-breaking a mustang. "A widow," he said again, feeling pleased.

"My husband was killed a year ago."

"Killed?"

"He was shot to death on Crescent range while riding alone, by a person or persons unknown."

"Too bad."

"Yes, too bad," Margaret said. "Steve Leland was a fine man. He was still young too — only thirty-two." Her lower lip quivered and tears glistened in her eyes. "And I miss him terribly, even after a whole year."

"The way I hear it, Crescent Ranch has a lot of enemies."

She blinked the tears away, and a hardness came into her face.

"That's what I want to talk to you about, Mr. Jernigan." Her voice too was suddenly hard. "You see —"

"Call me 'Ed,' why don't you?"

"All right — Ed. It's Crescent's enemies that I want to talk to you about, Ed. Since learning what kind of man you are, I've been wondering if you wouldn't hire on with me as a — well, as a range detective."

He stared at her. She was full of surprises, this lovely young widow. Suddenly wary of her, he said, "What kind of man is it you think I am?"

"The smart, tough kind that's not afraid of anything or anybody — and trustworthy to boot."

"I don't know, ma'am. I'm just —"

"Call me 'Margaret,' Ed. When you say 'ma'am,' it makes me feel like an old-maid schoolteacher."

"Well, Margaret, then . . . I'm just a poor, dumb galoot that hunts wild horses for a living. As a range detective, I'd be taking your money under false pretenses."

That wasn't exactly true. He had been a number of things besides a mustanger. He did know something of the cattle business, having grown up on a ranch and later worked as a cowhand. He had also spent a year with the Frontier Battalion. That had been after the Comanches stopped raiding and the Rangers had dealt only with cattle rustlers, horse thieves and other outlaws. In a pinch, he might do as a range detective. And he might also get himself killed playing at one.

"What would you expect of a man if he hired on as that?" he asked, merely out of curiosity. "For him to find out who killed your husband?"

"That would be a part of it," she said. "But I'm not sure such a thing would be possible. What I would really expect is for you to find out if I'm being cheated."

"Cheated how?"

"Out of my share of Crescent Ranch."

"You came into your husband's share on his death?"

She nodded. "I not only had a widow's rights, but he had the foresight to make out a will to make sure I received his estate."

"If it's all that iron-clad, how could you be cheated?"

"You'd have to know the situation at Crescent to understand."

"Well, tell me about the situation at Crescent," Jernigan said. "The telling shouldn't take longer than it takes me to get my breakfast and eat it."

30

"It's like this," Margaret said, frowning with thought as though needing to sort it out in her own mind. "Crescent Ranch was founded by old Matthew Leland. He came out from Texas some years ago with a herd of cattle and all his worldly goods. He was a widower then, and his two sons, Steve and Brad, were grown. Brad was the younger by two years, and natured differently from Steve. For one thing, he didn't like to work. For another, he had a yen to travel. One day he just drifted off. That was soon after they settled in the Territory. Matthew passed away a year later, after a brief illness, and Steve took over the operation of Crescent — and built it into a prosperous, fair-sized outfit.

"Two years ago he made a trip to Kansas City to deliver a beef herd. That was my home, and we met through a mutual acquaintance — the man who was head of the commission house that bought Steve's cattle. Because of me, Steve stayed on in Kansas City much longer than he had planned."

Margaret fell silent, and a faraway look came into her eyes.

He said, "Steve stayed on to court you, eh?"

She nodded. "Yes, to court me. And when he left, I went with him — as his wife. It was a good marriage. And I took to ranch life as though I'd never been just a town girl. We were happy, Steve and I. Too happy, maybe. Something had to go wrong, I suppose. Anyway, something did. Brad came home. After nearly five years with Steve not knowing where he was, he suddenly showed up — came home to stay, he said.

And he came too, of course, to claim his share of Matthew Leland's estate. He knew that old Matthew wanted Steve and him to share Crescent Ranch equally.

"As soon as he arrived, he demanded ten thousand dollars to pay some debts he had in San Francisco. At least, he claimed he owed that much money. One can never be sure when Brad Leland is telling the truth or lying. Anyway, Steve let him have the ten thousand — since Brad was half-owner of the outfit."

The waitress came, served Jernigan his breakfast and Margaret her coffee.

While Jernigan ate, Margaret continued to talk.

Brad Leland hadn't come alone, she explained. He'd brought along a wife, Kitty, a father-in-law, Ben Hazlitt, and a friend named Stace Barron. Margaret professed to like Kitty, to get along well with her. She claimed she rather liked Brad, as Steve had, despite his faults. Ben Hazlitt was a pompous, foolish man who enjoyed the life of ease he led at Crescent. All he seemed to want of life, Margaret told Jernigan, was three good meals a day, a comfortable bed, a plentiful supply of cigars and bourbon. But Stace Barron was something else again. Margaret's voice became barbed when she spoke of him.

"What have you got against him?" Jernigan asked.

"I can tell you that in a very few words," she said. "Since Steve's death, he acts as though he owns Crescent. Brad is completely under his influence, somehow. I suspect that he has some hold on Brad."

Jernigan's ham was so tough he suspected it had come from a javelina. While chewing on a piece of it, he studied the handsome young woman across the table.

"Then it's Barron you suspect of cheating you?"

"Well, yes."

"And of killing your husband?"

Margaret flinched at that, and for an instant her eyes mirrored the hurt brought on by the memory of her husband's murder.

Then, shaking her head, she said, "Barron was at Crescent headquarters when Steve was shot. I'm convinced it was an outsider who killed him. You see, Steve had enemies. He was a decent man, but he could be hard. He once had trouble with a man who fenced a waterhole that Crescent cattle used. Then there were people living off Crescent beef . . . Since there is no real law enforcement in these parts, Steve took the law into his own hands — as many cattlemen have done. When he caught a man butchering a Crescent steer, he used his fists on him . . . He would whip the man, then let him go. But when he caught a man running off cattle to sell . . . well, he took more severe measures to stop that sort of rustling. I know that he and the Crescent hands shot two such thieves and hanged a third. So he had enemies, Ed. I think he was killed by someone who wanted revenge."

"What about the range-grabbing folks say Crescent does?"

"Steve had no part in that," Margaret said. "Nor did his father before him. It's only since Brad — and Stace Barron — have been running the outfit that Crescent has taken to squeezing out the smaller ranchers. Brad talks of having a cattle empire, of being a cattle baron. But I'm sure that Barron put such notions into his head. Anyway, those two have given Crescent its bad name."

Jernigan finished his eggs and fried potatoes, but left what remained of the too-tough ham. He began drinking his coffee.

"Just how are you being cheated, Margaret?"

"There are so many ways a partner in a ranch can be cheated," she said. "I insist upon keeping a close watch on the books, but I can't know how honest the figures are that go into them. Brad could sell beef animals at a higher price than he enters in the accounts — and pocket the difference. I'm not saying he does that, you understand, but he could. He could also sell cattle without my knowing. Then there are the cattle on the range . . . Since Steve's death, I've registered my own brand. An M added to the regular Crescent quarter-moon. I've demanded that when calves are branded one be marked Crescent M for every one marked Crescent. I try to check. I do a lot of riding. I guess —" She smiled ruefully. "I guess I make a spectacle of myself, riding the range like a man. But for all my keeping tabs on the crew I can't be sure I'm getting all the calves that should be mine.

"And I can't trust the hands. Brad got rid of most of the old men, the ones who had been with Steve and before him with old Matthew. He hired others — and not riders from around these parts. He brought them from far off, and a rough, tough lot they are."

34

Jernigan gazed at her with admiration. For a city-reared girl, she was sure smart about the cattle business.

She went on, looking at him in an almost pleading way, "That's why I want to hire you as my private range detective, Ed. To find out if I'm being cheated on the sale of beef animals and on the calf branding."

Jernigan finished his coffee, brought out makings, and rolled a cigarette. He lit up and smoked thoughtfully for a moment, realizing that he was sorely tempted. But he knew he was being foolish in letting himself be tempted. Margaret Leland was offering to hire him, nothing more. And he didn't need money all that badly. Besides, he had long ago decided that there was only one boss he could abide — himself.

Sensibly, he put temptation behind him. Even if she were being robbed at Crescent Ranch, she was still a well-to-do young woman and therefore wouldn't want the likes of him, a back-country mustanger, calling on her with courting in mind.

She was watching him closely and seemed able to read his mind. "You won't do it?" she said, sounding distressed as well as disappointed.

"I'm sorry, but I don't think I'm the right man."

"I do, Ed."

He ignored that, and said, "What you ought to do is get in touch with the sheriff or even the U.S. marshal and ask one or the other to recommend an experienced range detective. Or you could contact the Pinkertons. They do that sort of work."

Margaret looked as though she didn't care for the advice, but before she could say more she was distracted by two men coming into the restaurant. Their boot heels struck sharp sound from the plank floor and their spurs gave off a musical jingle as they came toward the table where Jernigan and she sat. He recognized them as two of the three Crescent hands who had ridden up to the Alhambra Saloon.

A couple of hardcases, he decided. One was a burly man well on the way to middle-age, the other a kid not yet dry behind the ears but tough looking. Both were armed, and both moved with the arrogant swagger that marked the wild breed from ordinary cowhands. These two were the sort of riders Jernigan had heard were on Crescent's payroll.

The pair crowded right up to the table, the kid taking a stand at Jernigan's left elbow. That bothered the mustanger. He sensed that the two were primed for trouble, and he didn't like this one hovering over him. Most likely he would have to do something about it.

The burly one looked at Margaret with a wickedly amused grin, and said, "Ma'am, Mr. Barron sure has been worried because Pedro didn't get you home last night. He and us rode all the way into town just to find out what the holdup was. Reckon you sort of got tied up with this friend of yours, eh?"

Margaret looked at him coldly. "Kiley, you go back across the street and tell Mr. Barron to stay out of my affairs."

"He ain't going to like that, ma'am. His feelings will be hurt."

36

"You tell him, anyway."

"Now that's no way to act when he's worried about you, ma'am." Kiley's manner was openly disrespectful. He glanced at the young hand, still with a grin. "Is it, Tobie?"

Tobie chuckled. "It sure ain't, Russ. I figure we ought to show this friend of hers that he oughtn't to keep the lady away from home all night and cause Mr. Barron all that worry."

His hand came down on Jernigan's shoulder and gripped hard. The threat of violence and mayhem was here and Jernigan, taking into account both the odds against him and the disadvantage in his being seated, met it in the only way he could. He pressed the burning end of his cigarette hard against Tobie's hand.

Tobie howled with pain, jerked his burned hand away, jumped back. That same instant Jernigan shoved his chair back and heaved to his feet. He stared hard-eyed at young Tobie.

"You, sonny," Jernigan said. "You've insulted the lady and so owe her an apology.

"I ain't apologizing for saying what's true," the hardcase kid shot back. "She spent the night with —"

Jernigan hadn't done any soldiering and so wasn't aware of the rule that an offensive was the best defense. But his Ranger service had taught him that a surprise attack could do much to offset the disadvantage of even great odds. Before either of the Crescent men could carry out whatever move they had planned for him, he hit Tobie a backhanded blow to the face. The youth went reeling backward off balance, collided with a

37

table, toppled it over, and fell to the floor with it. Ignoring Russ Kiley, who was too flabbergasted to act at the moment, Jernigan went after Tobie, collared him, hauled him to his feet, and took a viselike grip on his right arm.

Tobie yelled, "Turn me loose, damn you! Turn me loose!"

Jernigan kept his hold on shirt collar and right wrist. He whipped the hardcase about to face Margaret Leland. She had remained seated at the table. She watched wide-eyed but without showing alarm. Her manner suggested that she expected nothing different than this of Ed Jernigan.

"Now, sonny," Jernigan said. "Let's hear you apologize like a nice boy."

Tobie cursed him. "Quit talking to me like I was a kid!"

Russ Kiley stood there, flat-footed, his mouth hanging open. A dull-witted sort, he was up against something unforeseen and didn't yet know how to cope with it. It was apparent to Jernigan that the man who had sent the pair to rough him up hadn't told them what to do if their intended victim reacted in this fashion.

Jernigan applied more pressure to Tobie's arm, causing the youth to whimper now. "Sooner or later, sonny, you're going to apologize to the lady. Better make it sooner."

"All right, damn you; I apologize!"

"You can do better than that," Jernigan told him, again applying pressure. "Say it like you mean it — and look at the lady when you do."

Tobie obeyed at last, looking at Margaret Leland and muttering, "I'm sorry, ma'am. I shouldn't have talked like that about you."

"That's a nice boy," Jernigan said, and with that spun him about and hustled him to the doorway and through it. He gave the youth a pitch that sent him sprawling to the dirt of the street. Going after him, he reached down and lifted Tobie's gun from its holster.

He turned back to the doorway at once, thrusting the captured gun into his waistband and drawing his own. He stepped into the restaurant with his long-barreled Colt's revolver cocked and leveled. This precaution proved wise, for Russ Kiley was waiting for him with a chair raised for a clubbing blow.

As Jernigan came through the doorway, Margaret called, "Ed, watch out!" She was on her feet now, looking as though she were trying to think of some way to keep the hardcase from using that chair.

Jernigan said, "Friend, I'll blow your fool head off before you can hit me with that. Now put it down — slow and easy."

Kiley swore under his breath but did as he was told. He stared at the mustanger with rage and hatred. He was feeling humiliated, and smarting badly.

Jernigan gestured with his gun. "Now unbuckle your gunrig and let it drop, so we have no senseless shooting that would leave one of us — meaning you — dead on the floor."

"Listen, you; I don't give up my gun for any man!"

Jernigan shot off his revolver, and the heavy report seemed to rock the room. He'd lowered his aim, put the slug into the floor at Kiley's feet. That was close enough for the hardcase. He dropped his gunrig, stepped away from it. Jernigan gestured toward the doorway.

"Outside with you," he said. "And don't lay for me. Try it, and my next shot will catch you dead-center in the chest."

Kiley moved wide around him to the doorway, muttering angrily under his breath. Jernigan eased the hammer of his gun off cocked position, holstered the weapon, and followed him outside. Kiley tried to duck away, but Jernigan put a hand to his back and gave him a violent shove. Russ Kiley went sprawling face-down in the dirt.

Jernigan looked around for Tobie and saw him limping along to the Alhambra Saloon. The youth was talking excitedly to the third Crescent rider, Steve Barron.

Now there's a horse of another color, Jernigan reflected as he settled his hard-eyed gaze on that one.

Barron was taking it all calmly enough. At least on the surface. He was lounging against one of the posts that supported the wooden awning of the saloon's porch. Puffing slowly on a cigar, he appeared totally unruffled by what had happened to the Crescent hands. He seemed not to be listening to the excited Tobie. He didn't even glance at Russ Kiley, who was now picking himself up out of the dirt. He simply looked across at Jernigan, and that with no expression at all.

The shot Jernigan had fired in the restaurant had brought people to the doorways of the business places and caused others to stop and stare on their way along the street. An aproned bartender was watching from the Alhambra's doorway. But Stace Barron acted as though there had been no gunshot and his companions hadn't been tumbled ignominiously into the street.

He was a darkly handsome man, and his clothes told that he was vain about his good looks. He was in riding garb, but not the sort worn by ordinary cowhands. His pearl-gray Stetson was store-new, his handsome hand-tooled black boots were bright with a recent polishing. His dark blue shirt was double-breasted and its twin rows of big buttons were mother-of-pearl. His black-and-brown gambler's pants fitted as though tailor-made. His gunrig was of black leather, and his gun had carved ivory butt plates.

His dudish appearance deceived Jernigan not at all. A man had only to take in Barron's pale, chill eyes, his nerveless calm, and his poker-game expression to know that here was no strutting Saturday night cowboy or mere barroom bravo — but a genuine gunman. And to Ed Jernigan the tag of gunman marked its wearer as the predator of the human race — a killer for profit or pleasure, or for both.

Jernigan felt his flesh crawl and the short hairs at the back of his neck bristle. But he told himself he would be damned if he would show that he was impressed, much less cowed, by the man.

His gaze steady on Barron, he called out, "You, mister; you sic your dogs on me another time, you'll find yourself wishing you'd kept them chained."

Barron's only reaction was to take the cigar from his mouth and spit into the street. It was a contemptuous

41

gesture that served notice on Ed Jernigan, far better than blustery words could have done, that he had Stace Barron for an enemy and had better watch out. Jernigan wasn't cowed by him, but he was impressed. He would indeed watch out from now on, and if he encountered Barron again, he wouldn't waste time trying to smooth things over with talk. Where the Steve Barrons of this world were concerned talk would only get a man killed. He would hold his tongue, grab for his gun, and maybe, just maybe, he would manage to stay among the living.

Because he needed Barron for an enemy no more than he needed another head, Jernigan suddenly wondered how he had gotten him for that. He knew, all right. It had come about because he had let his head be turned by a pretty face and a trim figure. Meaning Margaret Leland's, of course.

IV

Right then and there Ed Jernigan was gripped by a feeling — a hunch, a premonition, a something — that his carefree days had come to an end, thanks to the widow. He knew somehow that he hadn't seen the last of Stace Barron and those two hardcase Crescent hands. He wasn't at all happy about the prospect.

Turning from staring like a cross dog at his brand-new enemy, he found that the widow had been watching him and Barron from the restaurant doorway. He imagined that there was a satisfied, almost a jubilant gleam in her lovely amber-flecked brown eyes, and the unpleasant thought occurred to him that she was pleased with the enmity that had developed between him and Barron.

By damn, she's hoping I'll do him in!

Then he no longer saw that gleam, and wasn't sure it had been in her eyes at all. He told himself he must have been mistaken. She was too nice a lady, he wanted to believe, to want any man down in the dirt with his life ebbing away through the hole left by a .45 caliber slug.

"I'll get my hat and pay for my breakfast," he said, and she moved back from the doorway so he could enter.

The waitress was righting the chairs that had been knocked over when Tobie toppled the table. He gave her a hand with picking up the table, then paid her what he owed and added a sizable tip for the trouble his go-around with the Crescent hands had caused her. He picked up Kiley's gun, and took Tobie's from his waistband. He left both on the table, then retrieved his hat and rejoined Margaret.

"I'll see you to your rig, then head out," he told her. "Time I started for home."

"You're not hiring on with me, then?"

"Ma'am, I've got the feeling that if I don't stay out of Crescent's way I'll end up pretty dead — which I'm not eager to do."

"You're afraid of Stace Barron," she said, her tone accusing and making it seem he was the most despicable of cowards. "Well, it seems I was wrong about the sort of man you are."

"I reckon you were, ma'am," he said. "Because I sure am scared of that hombre, as it's only sensible to be."

She was angry with him, and bit her lower lip as though to hold back some nasty words she half wanted to use on him. She walked out of the restaurant, her head high, her shoulders squared, and her back stiff, looking angry in every inch of her. She turned along the street toward the fancy rig that waited, with the Mexican on the seat, in front of the hotel. Tagging along, he noticed that Stace Barron still lounged on the Alhambra's porch. Russ Kiley and Tobie were no longer in sight, and he supposed they were inside trying to forget they had been humiliated by sopping up rotgut whiskey.

Mel Harper came hurrying out of Burro Alley looking anxious about something. He was a skinny scarecrow of a man, as ugly as sin was supposed to be. He repped for the law, being Rincon's marshal as well as a deputy sheriff. He wasn't much account in either job, for he was all the law the town had. The county seat was sixty miles away, over yonder high mountains, and the sheriff, more politico than law officer, was evidently satisfied with his man in Rincon.

Harper said, "How do, Miz Leland. Howdy, Jernigan. Who fired that shot?"

Margaret merely nodded a greeting, while Jernigan, giving the badge-toter a blank look, said, "What shot?"

"A couple of minutes ago," Harper said. "I heard it plain as day. Somebody shot off a gun."

He was ineffectual as a lawman but officious of manner, and he sounded as though he really meant to do something about that shot. He hurried on along the street, intent upon finding the man who had disturbed the peace of his town.

"You see, Jernigan?" Margaret said. "There is a good example of why I can expect no help from the law."

Jernigan said, "Yes, ma'am," and then, as they arrived at the Crescent buggy, "Let me give you a hand, ma'am."

He hadn't failed to notice that they were no longer on a first-name basis. Theirs had been a pretty short-lived friendship.

He gave her a hand up, then stood by with his hat in his hand while she seated herself comfortably and arranged the long, full skirt of her dress to her satisfaction.

Then, looking at him, she said, "You won't change your mind?"

"No, ma'am. And I suggest again that you get in touch with the Pinkertons, since you can't count on me and don't have much faith in the law."

"Thank you," she said stiffly. "I may do that."

"There's just one thing I don't savvy, ma'am . . . How come you suspect that a man who worries when you don't get home on time is cheating you? It seems loco to me that he'd cheat somebody he cares all that much about."

As he spoke, Jernigan heard the clop-clopping of a horse being slow-walked along the street. Margaret looked toward the approaching rider and frowned with what seemed both dislike and annoyance. Guessing that the rider was Stace Barron, Jernigan looked around. He had guessed right.

Barron's mount was a big black that seemed closer to being a thoroughbred than a cow pony. It was long of leg and barrel. He reined it in at the side of the buggy where Jernigan stood, and the animal began a nervous prancing because it was so close to the rig. Ignoring Jernigan, Barron gazed steadily at the young woman.

"Margaret, everybody at Crescent was upset when you didn't get home last night."

She looked at him with that frown still marring her prettiness. "Everybody at Crescent should know that I'm able to look out for myself — and that I'm my own person to do as I please."

Jernigan saw Barron's dark, handsome face tighten up with the pressure of some strong emotion. He realized that the man had been able to hide his chagrin when his two companions were thrown into the street but couldn't conceal his feelings where Margaret Leland was concerned. Barron's reaction to her barbed words suggested that he believed he had a claim to her.

Jernigan knew that he might as well be on his way, but because of a contrary streak he wouldn't leave and let it seem that Barron's presence had driven him off.

Barron's horse kept up its nervous prancing this way and that, and the man did nothing to keep it under control. The animal's skittishness brought it closer and closer to Jernigan, and he, again contrary, refused to back away from it.

46

His gaze still steady on Margaret, Barron said, "There are always slick strangers to take in a woman traveling alone."

Margaret laughed. "My, my, you must take me for an innocent young thing." Her tone was mocking.

Stung, Barron flushed.

She dug the spur deeper, more cruelly. Looking at Jernigan, she said, "Are you that, Ed — a slick stranger who takes advantage of innocent women traveling alone?"

Jernigan grinned, but only with his mouth. He wasn't amused. He was now as wary of Margaret Leland as of the man, for she was baiting the two of them. He could only think that she wanted to bring about a clash between him and Stace Barron.

Barron at last took notice of him, with a black scowl. His horse did some more prancing, and again he did nothing to steady it.

Jernigan said, "Mister, you let that bronc crowd me any more you'll sure wish you'd shown better sense."

Stace Barron proved that he possessed a vulnerable spot such as no man who lived by the gun could afford. He had let himself be riled up by the woman, and because of his foul mood, he made the mistake of deliberately reining his mount in against Jernigan. Having anticipated such a move, Jernigan brought his hat up and slapped the animal on the nose with it. The black snorted with fright and began to buck.

Losing his temper completely, Barron swore and yelled, "Don't ever fool with another man's horse!"

He then made another mistake. He laid a hand on his gun as though about to draw it. That was a mistake because his mount was still acting up and also because he would have to bring the gun across the front of himself to line it on Jernigan. He hesitated as though aware that he wasn't set to use a gun. Then, perhaps due to his having been stung into a rage by the woman, he did make his draw.

Jernigan was on him the instant the weapon cleared its holster. He grabbed Barron by the left arm and pulled at him with all his might. The Crescent man was hauled halfway out of the saddle, and the black did the rest — bucked out from under him. Jernigan whipped him through the air, then let loose of him. Barron went sprawling into the dirt even harder than either Tobie or Kiley had done. He lay stunned, the breath knocked out of him. Jernigan kicked the gun from his hand, then picked it up and hurled it far across the street.

Gasping, looking dazed, Barron struggled to rise and made it to one foot and one knee. He held that pose, staring up at the mustanger with hate-filled eyes.

Jernigan said, "Friend, you sure bit off more than you can chew, didn't you now?"

Barron continued to stare at him, saying nothing. He just looked his rage and hatred, and his wish to kill. After a long moment he heaved to his feet and walked unsteadily to the now quieted black. He took his rage out on the animal, clubbing it between the eyes with his fist. The black snorted and shied away, but he grabbed its reins, hauled it about, and pulled himself to its saddle.

48

Looking at Jernigan again, he said, "You are a dead man," then reined the black roughly away and rode, still gunless, slowly along the street and out of town.

Jernigan picked up his hat, which he had dropped when jumping at Barron. He looked at Margaret Leland, and said, "If he comes gunning for me, I'll do what I must." His voice was abrasive with a sudden anger of his own. "But if I kill him, it won't be for you."

She flinched as though he had slapped her. "I never said or meant —"

He didn't wait to hear what she had never said or meant. He went around the buggy and into the hotel. He got his valise from his room and paid for his night's lodging. Coming outside again, he saw that the Crescent rig was on its way out of town. Looking after it, he had what he believed was his last glimpse of Margaret Leland.

Just as well, he told himself. *Bad medicine, her kind.*

Still angry, he headed for the Star Livery Stable to pick up the mount he had left there when El Paso-bound with his bunch of horses.

Two men perched on the fence of the corral adjoining the stable watched him come along the street. Recognizing them, he nodded in curt greeting. They were raggedy-pants cowmen from the Hatchet Hills, an old-timer named Pat Olgilvie and a younger man named Will Tolliver. He would have passed them without a word if Olgilvie hadn't spoken.

The old-timer said, "You should have killed him when you had the chance, Jernigan. You'd have been doing the whole range a mighty fine service."

Jernigan stopped in his tracks and stared at the pair, boiling mad. He swore, and said, "Everybody wants that hombre dead and me to do the killing. Has everybody gone loco all of a sudden?"

V

Jernigan's anger at these two was quickly gone. They'd always been friendly toward him, and he knew there was no real harm in them. If they wanted Stace Barron dead, it must be for good reason.

He set his valise down, took out makings for a cigarette, and asked, while shaping it, "Has that dude gunhand been giving you boys trouble?"

Pat Olgilvie snorted and spat tobacco juice to show in what low regard he held Barron.

Will Tolliver, a pipe-smoker, took his corncob from his mouth, and said sourly, "He finally got around to us, Ed . . . Gave each of us thirty days to gather our cattle and clear off the range. Crescent, he said, will pay us two hundred dollars each for our buildings — and then burn them."

Normally, Tolliver was an easy-going, mild-mannered sort, but he swore bitterly.

"Two hundred dollars!" he added. "Ain't a man's home his castle any more, that he can be ordered out of it and be thrown a little money as a sop?"

Jernigan would hardly have called Will Tolliver's one-room 'dobe a castle, but he did understand how the man felt about it.

50

"Look," he said, lighting a match with his thumbnail and firing his cigarette. "Why didn't you shoot him on the spot?"

Olgilvie gave a derisive guffaw of laughter. "Ed, if you lived on this range you wouldn't ask such a fool question. If there was a chance of any of us little ranchers shooting Barron, one of those Crescent has already driven out would have done for him. None of us is able to go up against a fast gun like him."

"He's not all that much of a terror. You two saw me roll him in the dirt when he had his gun in his hand."

"You, Ed," Tolliver said, pointing at him with the stem of his pipe, "are a different breed from us."

"Me?" Jernigan looked downright surprised. "I'm just another little man trying to scrape a living out of God's sometimes green earth."

"No, you're different," Tolliver said. "Pat and I heard about you going after those hardcases who held up the stage — and what you did when you caught them. And we sure did see you roll not only Barron but those other two Crescent hands as well in the dirt. I'm thinking that with you on our side we could give Crescent a good licking — make this Rincon Basin range safe for everybody."

Jernigan took a long drag on his cigarette, saying nothing.

Tolliver went on, "We small outfit men are holding a meeting up at San Miguel Saturday night. We aim to band together and try to find a way to make Crescent pull in its horns. I figure you'd be welcome to attend."

Olgilvie put in, "You'd better come, Ed. Because if that range-grabbing outfit clears the rest of us out of the Basin, it'll sure end up trying the same with you — even though you're living over on the edge of the Brenoso. And don't figure you'll just up and shoot that Stace Barron when the time comes — because he always rides up to a man's place with some of those tough Crescent hands siding him."

Jernigan said, "San Miguel, Saturday night. I'll think on it."

He picked up his valise and went into the livery stable for his mount.

Riding out ten minutes later, he did think about the meeting — and decided not to attend it. Those raggedy-pants cowmen would do a lot of talking and end up with some fool plan of action against Crescent that they wouldn't be able to carry out. Besides, he was a loner. He didn't believe in sitting in on a game in which other men dealt the cards. When Stace Barron got around to making trouble for him, as would surely happen sooner or later, he would do his fighting without calling on any of the Basin ranchers for help, no matter what the odds.

Reckon I do belong to a different breed — a damn fool breed of hombre . . . Else I wouldn't let a pretty woman get me into a bad fix with a couple of hardcases and a gun-hand.

The only part of the affair on which he could congratulate himself was his not having been seduced by Margaret Leland's feminine wiles into hiring on as

52

her personal, private range detective . . . Which would certainly have put him in an even worse fix.

Jernigan's ranch headquarters was located twenty-odd miles from Rincon, in a little valley rimmed by low hills. The east end of the valley opened into the *malpais*, where he did his mustanging, and he'd raised a pole fence at both ends to keep penned what horses he caught.

Letting himself through the gate in the west fence and seeing his buildings, a third of the way back through the valley, he felt glad to be home. His buildings weren't much, being just an adobe house and barn, but no matter how humble a man's home it was, as Will Tolliver had put it, his castle.

Seven horses grazed down the valley, and Jernigan saw that his only hired hand, Miguel Rojas, was working with a bronc in the breaking corral. Nearly seventy years old, Miguel had been a mustanger forever and could still top a wild one. Riding up to the corral, Jernigan saw that the old-timer had the horse, a blue roan stallion, gentled enough to rein it this way and that at will with the animal doing only a little rebellious bucking.

"Hey, *amigo* . . . . You've done a good job with that one."

Miguel grinned, pleased by the praise. "*Como 'stá*, Ed? All the fight is not out of him yet. He still likes to bite and kick, and I have to tie him to the snubbing post to saddle him. How was the trip? Did you get a good price for the horses?"

"The price was all right, and the trip was fine," Jernigan told him. "You should have come along, like I wanted you to."

Miguel shook his head. "No more trips to El Paso for me. I am still not over the last one."

They chuckled over the memory of that last trip. Miguel had gone across the Rio Grande to Juarez for a tequila binge. It had ended with his becoming involved in a *cantina* brawl and thrown into jail. Jernigan had gone over to pay his fine and found him much the worse for wear. Miguel had sworn never again, claimed he was getting too old to sow wild oats.

Getting down off the blue roan, he said, "And you managed to stay out of trouble, Ed?"

Jernigan had no desire to rehash his trouble during the stagecoach trip north from Lordsburg and in Rincon, but he told Miguel about both because he knew the old mustanger would enjoy hearing the tale.

"So now you have the Crescent outfit for an enemy, eh?" Miguel said. "But señora Leland . . . she is worth a little trouble, no?"

"Maybe she would be if a man figured on sparking her," Jernigan said. "Which I sure don't. You been doing any riding back in the Brenoso, *amigo?*"

"*Si* . . . And two days ago I saw the band of mustangs led by the big steeldust. The bunch that got away from us last winter by heading into the mountains. A lot of good young broncs with that steeldust."

"Where'd you spot them?"

"Over by the big *tinaja.*"

54

"*Bueno*," Jernigan said. "We'll ride out there in the morning and have a look."

In the morning, on their way to the *tinaja*, a rock-bound waterhole deep in the Brenoso, the horse Miguel was riding went suddenly lame and couldn't be ridden farther. He turned back on foot, leading the animal, and Jernigan went on alone.

Holding his mount, a zebra-striped dun, to a steady lope, Jernigan came to the waterhole somewhat before noon. He dismounted there, let the dun drink and graze while he cut for mustang sign. He found plenty, and his guess was that a band of wild horses had watered there last night. Steeldust's bunch, he hoped.

Their trail led southeastward on a meandering course, for they had grazed while moving slowly along, until it entered some sandhills. Here the animals — fourteen in number, by his tally of the hoofmarks — had moved at a faster pace. Beyond the hills, he trailed them through a broad rock field. Once out of this maze of giant boulders, huge slabs and towering spires, he followed the sign along the base of a steep escarpment. The mustangs had found a place where the debris of an ancient rockslide permitted an ascent, and he put his mount to climbing. Reaching the caprock, he found himself on a broad grassy mesa.

After a mile or so he topped a rise and saw the band grazing in the distance. He drifted toward them, slow-walking the dun and getting close enough to make out the big metallic-gray stallion that was the bunch-leader. The steeldust, always alert, became aware of him. It began circling the other horses, crowding in against them. Soon the stallion had them in motion. The bunch fled on southward at a run.

Jernigan reined in, grinning. *All right, Old Steeldust . . . run for it now, but I'll get you yet. That's a promise.*

Building a smoke, he watched the horses until they disappeared into a brush thicket far across the mesa. He turned back then, started for home. He arrived back at the west fence shortly before sundown and after riding a short distance into the valley came upon the first dead horse.

It was the blue roan that Miguel had been saddle-breaking yesterday. It had been shot in the head.

Reining in, Jernigan stared down at the dead animal uncomprehendingly for a long moment.

Thinking: *What the hell goes on here, anyway?*

He began to suspect, and riding on, began to know.

The second dead horse lay about fifty yards beyond the first. A little distance away, off to his right, two more lay dead. Farther away, down-valley, he saw the shape of three more down. He stopped by the second, and it too had been shot — once through the neck and again through the head. He knew he would find that the others had been killed in the same way, by gunfire.

He didn't go to have a look at the others, but lifted the dun to a run and headed for his buildings.

He hadn't time to be angry as yet, for he was thinking of Miguel — afraid he would find him, too, shot dead.

56

VI

Riding into the ranchyard and jerking the dun to a rearing halt, Jernigan saw first Miguel's lame horse dead in the main corral, the pen connected to the barn, and then Miguel himself sprawled on the ground in front of the house.

Ordinarily, Jernigan was too lighthearted a man to be profane but now, dropping from the dun, he swore bitterly. He was also too easy-going to be a hating man, but as he went to where the old-timer lay he was full of hatred as well as rage.

He knew whom to hate, of course.

The Crescent outfit.

Or, to narrow it down a bit, Stace Barron.

With some of the hardcased Crescent riders, Barron had come here looking for him and failing to find him had worked off his grudge — in part, at least — by killing the eight horses and old Miguel.

And now, by damn, he's got me for an enemy!

Jernigan figured, right then, that he had it in him to be a real mean enemy.

Miguel lay face-down, his body twisted — broken looking. Jernigan turned him over onto his back with care, just in case he was still alive. Miguel was. A groan escaped him, and he looked at Jernigan out of one eye. The left eye. The right one was swollen shut, and above it was a deep, bloody gash. The old-timer's nose was mashed, broken certainly. His lower lip was badly torn, as was his left ear. His right jaw was swollen, discolored. His entire face was a mess. He'd been battered unmercifully by savage fists, or maybe by a gun barrel. Jernigan's anger mounted, his hatred too.

"I'll get you inside, *amigo*. You hear me? You savvy?"

Miguel attempted a reply, but began to choke.

Another groan escaped him as Jernigan lifted him, telling of body injuries too. Being handled, even gently, was too much for him. He passed out, and was a limp, broken thing by the time Jernigan laid him on his bunk.

Jernigan gazed at him worriedly, not knowing what to do for a man who had been beaten to a pulp. After a moment he went to the kitchen end of the room and rummaged in the cupboard for the bottle of whiskey he kept on hand for medicinal purposes. While pouring some of the whiskey into a tin cup, he noticed that the house had not been touched. Barron and the men with him hadn't wrecked it, as Jernigan might have expected.

Not that there was much to wreck . . . The furniture was homemade of unpainted planks. Otherwise, there was only the fireplace, the cooking utensils, the tinwear off which Miguel and he ate, and a small stock of provisions.

Jernigan poured a few drops of whiskey into Miguel's slackly open mouth. He waited a moment and then let a few more drops trickle down his throat. Finally Miguel came around, looked at him with his one good eye.

"Try to drink a little more of this, *amigo* . . . . For a painkiller."

Miguel drank a little more, then quite a lot more.

Jernigan got a basin of water, a washrag, a clean flour sack. Ever so gently, he washed Miguel's battered face clean of blood.

"I hurt deep inside, Ed," he said feebly. "I think I have cracked ribs for one thing. What else, I do not know."

"I'll bandage you up tight, then take you to Rincon to the doctor."

"I can't sit a horse, Ed."

"I'll ride to Will Tolliver's place, borrow his wagon, and haul you to town."

While bandaging him about the middle, Jernigan asked, "They were Crescent hands — one of them a real dude?"

"They rode horses branded with a quarter-moon," Miguel said. "And, *sí*, one was dressed too fine to be a ranchhand. The others were tough hombres — not ordinary ranchhands, either."

"How many of them?"

"Four. They caught me in the corral, rubbing liniment on the claybank's game leg. They wanted to know where you were. When I said you were gone deep into the Badlands, they covered me with their guns. The dude shot the claybank, then rode out and shot our other horses. When he came back, he told the others to take hold of me. Two grabbed me. The one had a scar all the way across the left side of his face. The other was young, hardly more than a *muchacho*."

"That one I know," Jernigan said. "Tobie by name."

"Then the dude —"

"He's the gunhand I told you about — Stace Barron."

"*Sí*. He said I was to tell you to clear out of this valley, because it is now a part of Crescent range. He also said that if you don't leave, you will be killed."

"Then they worked you over?" Jernigan said, his voice harsh with his rage and hatred. "On Barron's orders?"

"That is so," Miguel said. "On that one's orders. The two held me, and a big, red-faced hombre used his fists on me." He shuddered with the memory of the beating. "I thought he would kill me, that big hombre."

"Russ Kiley," Jernigan said, more to himself than to the old man. "Barron, Tobie, Kiley, and one with a scarred face. I'll be looking them up by-and-by." Then, directly to Miguel: "You keep still, take it easy. I'll go after Tolliver's wagon."

"Maybe I will be all right without seeing a doctor."

"That's not likely, the shape you're in," Jernigan told him, and went out to his horse.

Once out of his little valley, he had a half dozen miles to ride. He pushed the dun hard the entire way, darkness closing down on the range before he'd covered half the distance to Tolliver's ranch. He rode with hard thoughts, realizing that his free and easy days were now in the past. From tonight on he would have to fight for his ranch — and even to stay alive.

All because I let a pretty woman go to breakfast with me.

But he knew that even if Stace Barron should let up on him now, which wasn't likely, he would have no peace of mind until he had settled accounts on the gunhand for the beating Miguel had been given and for those eight dead horses. That was just something a man couldn't take. To Ed Jernigan's mind, the man who turned the other cheek wasn't much of a man.

Finally he saw a light ahead, the lamplit window of Will Tolliver's ranchhouse.

Pulling up short of the yard, Jernigan called out, "It's Ed Jernigan, Will."

"Come on in, Ed. You're riding late. What's up?"

"Trouble with Crescent. I was away from my place when Barron and some others showed up. They beat old Miguel nearly to death. I'd like to borrow your wagon, to take him to the doctor at Rincon."

"I'll hitch up for you. But first I'll have to go looking for my wagon team. You had supper?"

"Only breakfast all day."

"Coffee on the fire," Tolliver said. "Some leftover biscuits and beans. Go in and help yourself. I'll get the harness nags ready."

Jernigan dismounted, led the blowing dun over to the corral, off-saddled it, and turned it into the pen.

"I appreciate this, Will."

"Neighbors," Tolliver said, as though that explained everything.

Going to the house, Jernigan reflected that there were neighbors *and* neighbors. Crescent's kind played hob with a range, and every range seemed to have a Crescent outfit. Trouble, always trouble.

He struck a match and lit the oil lamp that hung from the ceiling. This house itself was no different from

61

his own, but Will Tolliver had two pieces of furniture — a bed and a rocking chair — that were not homemade. He also had several framed pictures on the walls, and a shelf crowded with books. A man who had certainly known a different life at one time, Will Tolliver.

Jernigan went to the fireplace, where a bed of embers still glowed bright red, and filled a tin cup with coffee. He found the leftover biscuits and beans on the table and, sitting down, helped himself. After eating, he rolled a cigarette and sat smoking until hearing Tolliver come in with the wagon team. Going outside then, he lent a hand with hitching the horses to Tolliver's light spring wagon and afterward got his rifle from his saddle on the corral fence to take along on the trip to Rincon.

"Just in case I run into some Crescent hands," he said, climbing to the wagon's seat.

Handing him the reins, Tolliver said, "Well, you're one of us now, Ed. You'll come to the meeting Saturday night, won't you?"

"I may at that," Jernigan said, rein-slapping the horses into motion. "And I'll bring this rig back tomorrow, Will."

He hauled into Rincon soon after sunup, and a sleepy Mel Harper came from his box-sized office as the Tolliver horses plodded along the main street.

"What happened? Who's that you're hauling?"

Jernigan's opinion of the local law was no better than Margaret Leland's, and he didn't stop to explain.

"My hired hand, Miguel Rojas," he called back. "I'm taking him to Doc Harvey."

62

The doctor had his office and living quarters over Barton's Mercantile, and Jernigan, after pulling up alongside the building, lifted Miguel from the bed of the wagon and carried him up the flight of open stairs. He kicked at the door when reaching the landing, and kept kicking it until it was opened.

Dr. Harvey was a young man who wore a neatly trimmed beard to look more mature and to inspire confidence. He was in his nightshirt but had pulled his pants on over it, leaving the suspenders to dangle, and thrust his feet into carpet slippers.

"Take it easy, Jernigan," he grumbled. "I was up at San Miguel delivering twins and have hardly been to bed." Then, gazing at the man in Jernigan's arms with professional interest: "A horse threw him, and he got dragged when his foot caught in the stirrup. Right? Well, bring him in. Don't just stand there."

"Doc," Jernigan said, "you're in a worse temper than I am — and I've got more trouble than you'll know in your lifetime."

He carried Miguel through the doctor's waiting room and office to a room with a long, narrow table. On Harvey's orders, he laid the old man on the table and began undressing him.

"He was beaten, eh?"

"He was — by a real ornery cuss."

"Plenty of them around," Harvey said, bending over the patient. "What's your name, friend?"

The long wagon trip had left Miguel in poor shape, and he seemed not to understand the question.

"His name is Miguel Rojas," Jernigan said. "He works for me — hunts mustangs with me. Helps break them too. He's a damn good man, for his age."

"Where does he complain of hurting, aside from about the face?"

"In his left side. Cracked ribs, he figures. He said, too, last night that he hurts deep inside."

"You had breakfast, Jernigan?"

"No. And haven't given it a thought."

"Well, go get some," Dr. Harvey said. "I don't want you hovering over me while I'm working on him."

Jernigan gave him a sourly amused look. "You are a mean-tempered man, all right, Doc," he said, and left the room.

He had breakfast at the Welcome Café, and afterward walked to the marshal's office. Mel Harper sat at his desk reading a wanted dodger that evidently had just come in the mail. His homely face was set with concentration and his lips moved with each word he puzzled out. Finally he looked up, and frowned.

"Oh, it's you, Jernigan," he said. "I've got a crow to pick with you. You're the hombre who fired that shot the other morning. And you rode out of town before I found out it was you."

"If you found that out, you must have found out why I fired it," Jernigan said. "I wasn't letting that Crescent hardcase crown me with a chair. Anyway, that's water over the dam. I'm here about what happened to Miguel."

"Well, what did happen to him?"

"Stace Barron and three other Crescent men came to my ranch yesterday. When they didn't find me there, Barron shot eight of my horses and had his hardcases beat Miguel to within an inch of his life."

"What makes you so sure it was Barron and some other Crescent men?"

"Why, man, Miguel told me."

"The way he looked when you hauled him in, he was in no shape to be sure of that or of anything else."

Jernigan stared at him with disgust. "You're saying the man doesn't know who gave him that roughing-up?"

"It'd be his word against that of Barron and the others, remember," Harper said. "Now if Miguel had a witness or two it'd make a lot of difference. Still, he can sign a complaint against them. So can you, for the horses that were killed, if you like."

"And then what?"

"Then I'd have to arrest them, being a sheriff's deputy as well as town marshal. I'd take them to jail at the county seat. They'd post bond, no doubt, but later there would be a trial and —"

"Forget it," Jernigan said, and turned abruptly to the door. From there, he added bitingly: "I can see that a man gets no help from the law in these parts. So I'll just settle with Crescent in my own way."

"Now hold on," Harper said, heaving out of his chair and putting on his officious mien. "You can't take the law into your own hands. Besides, you'll end up one sorry hombre if you buck that outfit."

"So long, Marshal," Jernigan said, and went out.

He was sore about Harper's lack of enthusiasm for keeping the peace in his bailiwick only for so long as it took him to return to Dr. Harvey's office. He hadn't actually expected that badge-toter to do anything about the beating of Miguel or the killing of those eight horses. After all, the law hadn't done anything about a more serious matter — the range war Crescent was waging against the two-bit ranchers.

VII

Jernigan got back to Will Tolliver's place shortly before sundown. Supper-fire smoke was rising from the chimney of the adobe house. Tolliver appeared at the door and watched him drive the rig across the yard and pull up alongside the barn.

Taking his corncob pipe from his mouth, he called, "How's Miguel doing?"

"The doc patched him up and said he'll be as sound as a dollar in a few weeks," Jernigan told him. "I found a place for him to stay, with a widow woman in the Mex part of town. She promised to take good care of him. I'll put up your horses, Will."

"Just turn them loose on the range," Tolliver said. "Then come in and have supper. It's about ready."

When entering the house, Jernigan carried a square pound can of tobacco. He set it on the table.

"London Fancy Pipe Mixture," he said. "Asa Barton at the Mercantile said it's what you smoke. For the loan of the wagon and team."

"You didn't owe me anything, but — *muchas gracias*."

Jernigan hung his hat and gunrig on a wall peg, then went out back to wash up.

Returning to the kitchen, he said, "I'll be at that meeting Saturday night."

Tolliver nodded, and sounding pleased, said, "I thought you would. I rode over to Pat Olgilvie's today and told him I figured we could count on you to join us little ranchers against Crescent now. I for one will be glad to have you, Ed. Our crowd needs a man who knows how to fight. Sit down, and I'll dish out the grub."

They seated themselves at the table, and ate in the usual way of their kind, foregoing conversation to give the whole of their attention to the food. After the meal, Tolliver filled his pipe with the new tobacco and Jernigan rolled a cigarette.

As he lit up, Tolliver said, "You may as well bunk here tonight, Ed. You didn't get any sleep last night, and it's a long ride to your Slash J Ranch."

Jernigan said, "I'll take you up on that, Will," for he had been dreading saddling up his dun and making the ride to his own place.

In the morning he headed for home right after breakfast, holding the dun horse to an easy lope as the sun appeared above the mountain peaks. It was a fine day, with the soft early light giving the land a fleeting golden glow. The kind of day, he reflected, that made a man feel glad he was alive — even when weighted down by trouble.

Trouble.

He hadn't anticipated Crescent's striking at him again so soon. But upon riding through the narrow gap in the hills into what he regarded as his own little valley he found that outfit wasn't giving him any respite from trouble.

His west fence was down.

He reined in, stared with disbelieving eyes. But it was true enough. The pole fence that Miguel and he had raised during a couple of weeks of hard toil had been pulled down from one end to the other — no doubt by riders attaching their catch-ropes to the posts. Those riders had even dragged the wreckage aside and made a pile of it.

Trouble was making a profane man of Ed Jernigan. He swore aloud, resoundingly. Gazing out across the valley, he saw a bunch of cattle had been driven in there and were already scattered about as they grazed. Crescent cattle, of course. He knew that without riding out there and having a look at their brand.

Four horses grazed near the buildings. They, too, would be wearing the quarter-moon brand, and their owners, Crescent hands, would be making themselves at home in his house.

Riding on, slowly and with his rifle across his saddle, he saw that they had removed the dead claybank from the corral attached to the barn — dragged it off somewhere. That showed they intended to stay there.

Not for long will they! Jernigan promised himself.

A man was lounging in the doorway of the house, watching him approach. He spoke over his shoulder, afterward stepping out from the doorway. The others came outside. Two of the four remained by the house. The other two crossed the yard and stood by the barn.

Jernigan's rage was a savage thing but it didn't cause him to throw caution aside. He pulled up short of the yard, telling himself he wasn't so loco mad that he would ride into a crossfire.

He gave each of the four a good, hard look. They were strangers to him, but he knew them for the same toughhand breed as those two Crescent riders he had tangled with in the restaurant at Rincon the other morning. They were not run of the mill cowhands.

He said, "Crescent figures on keeping this for a line camp, does it?"

"It sure does," one of them replied. "Are you Jernigan?"

"I am."

"Well, Mr. Jernigan, sir, you're just out of luck," the spokesman for the four said, his tone mocking. "If you want to move your personal belongings out, you're welcome to do it. Otherwise, ride along. This valley is now part of Crescent range — and Crescent is a cross-dog outfit that doesn't take to trespassers."

It took some doing, but Jernigan kept a tight rein on his temper. A wrong move now, and he would end up a dead man. He might nail one or even two of them, but not all four. He would take their guff, let them brand him the trespasser — for now. As for his personal belongings . . . he had all his savings hidden away in the barn, in what he hoped was a safe place. Twenty-two hundred dollars in gold and silver specie. But he wasn't trying to take it away now. Later, but not now. He didn't doubt for a second that Stace Barron had given these hardcases orders to do him in if they got the chance.

"I'll just leave my belongings," he said. "Because I'll be coming back here — and you'll be leaving."

"Don't be in a hurry about it, Mr. Jernigan, sir," the one said, and the others burst into raucous laughter.

Jernigan said no more, but then turned away. He watched over his shoulder, but none drew on him. Probably because the range was long for their handguns but not for his rifle. When well away from the yard, he turned past the rear of the barn and lifted his horse to a run — and ran it toward the four grazing Crescent mounts.

These horses had been turned loose unsaddled, and he was able to start them running by crowding in on them with loud yells. He drove them west through the valley, kept them moving toward the gap in the hills. When they were well on their way, he swung his dun about and reined it in.

As he had expected, his taking their horses drew a reaction from the Crescent men. They came running out from the buildings, their guns in their hands. As he had known, nothing upset riding men so much as losing their mounts.

He brought his Winchester to his shoulder and squeezed off three shots as fast as he could work trigger and lever. The range was now long even for a rifle, and he didn't count on hitting any of them. But he hoped his shooting would throw a scare into them. It seemed to do just that. The four scurried for what cover was handy — rocks, bushes, gullies. A couple of them cut loose with their handguns, but the slugs came nowhere near him.

He rode on, and catching up with the Crescent horses, drove them through the hills onto the open country of Rincon Basin. He then dismounted in the gap, in plain sight of the four men below, to make sure they didn't set out on foot after their mounts. He hunkered down with his back to a boulder, rolled and lit a cigarette, and wondered: *What now?*

He didn't know what his next move should be. This was a stalemate, a Mexican standoff. All that was clear to him was that, any way he looked at it, the odds were still four to one against him.

The hardcases didn't know what to do about the situation, either. But they didn't need to do anything, he reflected with some bitterness. They had only to sit tight. They held his buildings, and at mid-day, when the smoke of a cook-fire rose from the chimney of the house, he was reminded that they held his store of provisions as well. They would be dipping into it, he was sure, even though having packed in some grub from Crescent.

They merely had to sit tight and outwait him. Sooner or later hunger would drive him away. But not yet . . . Not until he had harassed them some more.

At sundown, when smoke again rose from the house chimney, telling that the four were rustling up evening chuck, hunger was gnawing at his belly. Still he stuck it out, and finally, as dusk thickened into darkness, he went to his horse, tightened its cinches, and rose to the saddle. He rode down into the valley and swung along the base of the hills to the south.

The night was thickly dark, and he had to depend on his memory to sort out the lay of the land. When figuring he was some distance beyond the buildings, he turned away from the hills and rode into the valley until he came to the creek that flowed in a meandering course through it. Here he dismounted, let the dun drink, then tied it among some bushes.

Bellying down at the stream, he, too, drank and then, carrying his rifle, walked to a slight rise of ground to the southeast of the buildings. From the crest of the rise he could see the lamplit windows of his house.

Taking a prone position, he lined the Winchester's sights on one of the two windows and began a slow, methodical shooting. He shot out its panes — and, he hoped, threw a scare into the men in the house.

He had no sooner gotten off three shots when gunfire from the darkness beyond the buildings let him know he hadn't caught them off guard. Using rifles, two of the four drove some lead in his direction — having spotted the muzzle flashes of his weapon. One was a little distance south of the house and barn, the other as far north. They had expected his attack, and so his sniping had failed to throw a scare into them — had gained him nothing.

He shifted his aim to try for the man to the south. He drove a slug at the spurt of powderflame from that one's rifle, then immediately fired twice more. No more shots came from there at once, but the man to the north kept up his fire. He put his slugs so close that Jernigan, hearing the shriek of them, hugged the ground.

While pinned down, Jernigan wondered about the other two hardcases. Their not taking part in the shooting was making him uneasy.

The man to the south got off another shot, from a new position. Jernigan again fired at the flash of his rifle, but again had no feeling that he'd scored a hit. The other rifleman opened up again, no doubt after having reloaded his weapon. Jernigan had a try at him. Another wasted cartridge, for both Crescent men now laid down a hot and heavy fire on his position.

He scrambled back from the crest of the rise, out of harm's way. He hated to admit it, but he'd made a fool play in coming down into the valley. These men weren't the sort to be unnerved by the long-range sniping of a single gun in the dark. Quite likely they'd played this sort of game before — and equally likely they were trying to box him in. The two who were doing no shooting had to be somewhere about — but not in the ranchhouse, where the lamp still burned. They could be sneaking up on him right now.

Down off the rim, Jernigan stopped for a moment to listen into the inky darkness. The pair with the rifles had stopped shooting, and the night was utterly silent for the moment.

That moment passed, and he heard a faint sound of movement somewhere near. Over in the bushes fringing the creek, he thought. He sank to the ground.

A furtive voice called out, more loudly than its owner realized, "You see him, Red?"

Jernigan didn't catch the reply, but was sure there had been one. He was equally sure now that the four Crescent hands had counted on his making a play tonight and set a trap for him. A trap in which he'd come very close to being caught.

Come to think of it, I will be caught in it — if I don't spot these two before they do me.

The next instant the voice he'd heard before said, "The sneaky son must still be on that rise. Come on."

He placed them now, off to his right. To bring his rifle to bear in that direction, he had to change his position. As he moved one of the pair spotted him.

"There he is! Get him! Nail the son!"

A gun opened up — a Colt's .45, by the heavy blast of it. The man firing it was no slouch with a revolver, either. Again the range was long for a handgun, but the slug struck so close it kicked dirt into Jernigan's face.

VIII

Jernigan realized he had left to him only the time it took the still unseen Crescent man to thumb back the hammer of his gun and steady the weapon for a second shot — which wouldn't be a miss.

He acted in that split second of time, squeezing off a shot of his own and then heaving over in a frantic roll. His shot did not find its mark, but it did rattle the hardcase and keep him from shifting his aim. When the

74

handgun fired again, its slug struck the ground at the spot that Jernigan had just vacated.

He flung himself into another roll, jacking a fresh load into the Winchester's chamber while in motion. His heart was slamming against his rib cage, and there was a hollow feeling in his gut — not hunger now, but honest fear. He had the acrid smell of burnt powder in his nostrils, and the taste of it in his mouth. His vision was uncertain from the flashes of muzzle flame, and when he fired his second shot, it was blindly. Having fired it, he threw himself into yet another roll.

Two guns blasted now, their slugs probing for him. His third wild heaving dropped him into a shallow gully, which gave him some slight protection. He worked the rifle's lever once more, readying a third shot.

One of the hidden pair burst out, "I think we nailed him!" He sounded jubilant.

The other said, his tone low and wary, "Don't move. He could be playing 'possum."

Jernigan lay doggo in the gully, waiting for his vision to clear. He finally removed his hat, tossed it aside, raised his head slightly. Without being aware of it, he was holding his breath and there was an aching tightness in his chest. His heart was still pounding hard. His mouth had gone dry, while moisture gathered on his brow and on his palms.

He caught a hoarse whisper: "You see him, Red?"

And another: "No, but I know where he is. Cover me, and I'll smoke him out — if he's still alive."

Jernigan saw a shadowy figure now. It emerged from the bushes, bent low. He saw too the glint of a gun barrel. The figure sank to the ground, began crawling in his direction. In a moment the Crescent man would be on his flank and, spotting him, have an easy target.

Jernigan waited no longer. Ignoring the second man, the one still hidden, he fired squarely into the crawling figure. That one uttered a startled yelp, and his gun went off unaimed. Jernigan readied another shot, but realized it was not needed there. The hit man was still on the ground.

The other hardcase called out in alarm, "Red? You all right, Red?"

He lacked the nerve of the one who had been shot, and now, as Jernigan fired in his direction, he took flight — crashing through the bushes, splashing across the creek. Jernigan drove another shot after him, to keep him running through the darkness.

Jernigan, retrieving his hat and rising from the gully, felt no pity for the dead man. To his mind, men who hired on for fighting wages, as these Crescent hands had doubtlessly done, deserved having no tears shed over them when they were paid off in lead. He moved off, headed upstream of the creek to where he'd left his horse.

Mounting the dun, he rode out of the valley the same way he had come into it. He went through the hills and struck out for Will Tolliver's ranch, for the second night riding with anger roiling in him.

Tonight however his anger was tempered by uneasiness, because of the tremendous odds he was bucking. He had spilled Crescent blood in his first fight with the outfit, but he had no reason to be elated. At the moment he felt that in taking on Stace Barron and his hardcased crew he had bitten off more than he could chew.

He hadn't any choice but to go on fighting, though. Unless he cut and ran for it.

But, by damn, I'm not a running man!

Tolliver's ranchhouse was dark when he approached it this time, but the man himself was alert. Tolliver either slept very light or hadn't yet been asleep. He replied to Jernigan's hail at once.

"Come on in, Ed."

Jernigan rode across the yard, reined in by the house. "Sorry if I disturbed your sleep, Will."

"You didn't. I was doing some reading."

There was a light inside. Gunny-sack curtains at the windows kept it from being seen from outside — and kept anyone from seeing in, from taking a shot at the occupant of the house.

"More trouble, Ed?"

Jernigan told him what he'd found that morning at his Slash J Ranch and what had happened since.

With a wry smile, he ended up, "So I'm looking for a room and board. Want to put me up for a while?"

"Be glad to have you," Tolliver said. "Off-saddle your bronc and come on in. I'll throw some wood on the fire and heat up some grub."

A loner Jernigan might be, but now he was grateful he knew a man friendly enough to take him in. When

77

they were seated at the table, Jernigan dug into the food with a right good will.

Puffing on his pipe, Tolliver said, "They didn't give you any deadline for moving out — or offer to pay for your buildings? They just took over?"

"That's it. My place is now a Crescent line camp — they claim."

"They've treated you harder than the rest of us, Ed."

"Because Stace Barron has a personal grudge against me," Jernigan said. "He figured I was playing up to the Leland woman, and so sicced those two toughhands, Tobie and Kiley, on me. Then he tried to make me eat crow, himself — and got rolled in the dirt. A blow to his pride, that. A festering sore that could only be healed by his breaking me. Maybe he's trying to goad me into coming gunning for him — and hopes he'll have the edge when and if I do."

"Is she his woman, do you think?"

Jernigan shook his head. "He wishes she was — hopes she will be. As for the lady, she claims to hate the sight of him."

"And there's nothing between you and her?"

"Nope. I only got to know her through being on the stage that was held up. When I returned what the holdup men got from her, she had the notion I might hire on as her private range detective — to find out if she's getting her fair share of Crescent's profits and calf crop. No, sir," Jernigan added with emphasis. "There's nothing between Margaret Leland and me."

"And yet all your trouble," Tolliver said, marveling, "came about because of her."

Briefly, Jernigan flashed his old devil-may-care grin. "Which proves a man should never be taken in by a pretty face and a trim ankle. Anyway, not a dumb back-country hombre like me." Then, his grin gone and his face turned rock-hard: "I'll be doing some troublemaking of my own — for Crescent — before long. Or for Stace Barron, at least. He'll know he's in a fight, believe me."

"Maybe you'll have plenty of help after the meeting Saturday night," Tolliver said. "There will be a couple dozen men on hand who have as much reason to hate Crescent as you have — and that includes me. You side us, Ed, and we'll side you."

"Fair enough," Jernigan said, but he looked and sounded a bit dubious that it would work out that way.

IX

Accompanied by Will Tolliver and Pat Olgilvie, Ed Jernigan rode into San Miguel at dusk Saturday night.

Located at the extreme northern end of Rincon Basin, this was an ancient adobe town and still mostly Mexican. Some of the Basin ranchers came there to trade, and to have an occasional night of fun. A wide-open town, it also attracted riders from other parts. A full quota of *cantineros*, monte dealers, and dark-eyed *señoritas* was always on hand to relieve such gentry of their money. Jernigan visited the place once in a while, when in the mood for some lively sport.

The ranchers against whom Crescent was waging its range war had arranged with one of the *cantina* owners to hold their meeting in his establishment. All other patrons would be barred during the evening.

Two dozen or more men were in the *cantina*, most bellied up to the bar and the others seated at tables. A noisy babel of voices indicated that a lot of red-eye whiskey had already gone down the hatch. The *cantinero*, hugely fat and having a *bandido* moustache, had a man helping him behind the bar and another waiting on tables. A blue haze of tobacco smoke shrouded the hanging oil lamps. The place reeked with the smell of beer and liquor.

Jernigan spotted a vacant table at the rear of the long, narrow room and led the other two men to it.

"I'll buy a bottle," he said, feeling himself in Tolliver's debt if not Olgilvie's. "*Muchacho* . . . . Over here!"

When the waiter came, he ordered a bottle of whiskey, three glasses, and a half dozen thin, black Mexican cigars. By the time he was served, several more men had come into the place.

Passing the cigars around and pouring the drinks, he said, "Must be thirty men here. Enough to scare that range-grabbing outfit out of the Basin — if they stick together and make a show of strength." He pushed one drink across to Tolliver, one to Olgilvie, and lifted the third. "Here's to some good coming of this get-together."

The three of them drank to that, and he choked, almost strangled, on the swallow he took. It wasn't the

80

whiskey that caused him the discomfort, however. Rather, he received a bad jolt from seeing Matt Baylor among the men at the bar.

He told himself he must be mistaken, that it was somebody who just looked like the stage robber. Then the man turned, a mug of beer in his hand and a broad convivial grin on his face. It was Matt Baylor, all right.

I'll be damned, Jernigan thought. *Rubbing elbows with honest men, bold as brass.*

Baylor was big and burly, rough and tough looking, and yet no different in appearance from the other men in the place.

Or from me, Jernigan told himself, realizing that this bunch, like a group of hard-working ranchers anywhere, was a pretty scruffy lot.

He continued to stare at Baylor, and finally the stage robber, his gaze drifting about the room, looked directly at him. If the man was taken aback by seeing him there, he showed no signs of it. Instead, his gaze remained steady and his grin actually widened. And he raised his beer mug in salute.

Jernigan muttered, "Well, that beats all."

Olgilvie and Tolliver looked at him wonderingly, and the latter asked, "What's wrong, Ed? You look like you've seen a ghost."

"That hombre with his back to the bar — Matt Baylor . . . does he live in the Basin and have cattle on the range?"

Both of the men at the table with him nodded, and Tolliver said, "Sure, Ed. He's one of us. He's partners with Jake Whittaker, and they have a spread north of the Hatchets. They run a few hundred head of stock. Baylor leaves the ranching to Whittaker and goes off to work at jobs a lot of the time. He was freighting out of Lordsburg for a spell, and before that swinging a pick and a shovel in a mine at Silver City. A man with a lot of get up and go, Matt Baylor. What troubles you about him?"

Jernigan debated with himself for a moment and decided he couldn't brand Baylor a stage robber now, when he hadn't done so earlier. The time to have done that had been when he arrived at Rincon after his gunfight with the holdup trio. He wouldn't be able to make such a charge stick at this late date, for Baylor would naturally deny it — and one man's word was as good as another's.

Baylor evidently figured it that way too, since he was all set to brazen it out. In fact, he showed no sign that he even feared that Jernigan would make such a charge against him.

The loco part of it was, Jernigan thought, the man had grinned at him and raised his glass to him in *compadre* fashion . . . as though there had been no stagecoach holdup, and no gunfight. And as though he, Ed Jernigan, hadn't killed Baylor's brother.

To Will Tolliver, Jernigan said, "It's nothing. I just didn't know that hombre was a cowman."

He pushed the bottle across to Pat Olgilvie, who had emptied his glass, then lit a cigar and, while smoking it, let his gaze drift about the room. He wondered about the others. Olgilvie and Tolliver were honest men, so far as he knew. He supposed that most of the rest of these ranchers were also that.

Jernigan made up his mind about one thing. He wasn't about to trust any of these men too far, or even count on them to help him get his ranch back. If there was one bad apple in the barrel, there could be others, maybe not all dishonest like Baylor, but the weak, the stupid and the foolhardy. He would have to do his fighting alone. With the meeting not yet even called to order, Jernigan was wishing he hadn't bothered to attend it. He could have done himself more good by going back to his valley and drawing the Crescent men there into another round of gunplay.

Finally the meeting was opened, the man acting as chairman being Colonel F. X. Mowbrey. He was a white-haired, one-armed veteran of the Civil War. He had lost his left arm at Gettysburg. Jernigan was acquainted with him, considered him a decent sort. Mowbrey's two sons helped him work his ranch. They were present now, standing over at the bar.

The colonel spoke of the nine ranchers who had been removed from the Basin by the Crescent outfit, in one way or another.

"Four were scared off," he said, warming to his subject and becoming somewhat emotional. "Crescent's hired gunman, backed by a hardcased crew, ordered them to leave. Fearing for their lives, they gathered their cattle, packed their belongings, and moved away. Two of the others were murdered by Crescent hands, and one was gunwhipped so severely he is now a helpless cripple. Two simply disappeared, and I suspect they were shot dead in some lonely place where their bones will one day be found.

"Others of us are now the victims of this vicious outfit. I, for one, have been given one month to leave the range — or suffer the consequences. To add insult to injury, I have been told I will be paid a mere two hundred dollars for my buildings. Pat Olgilvie and Will Tolliver have also been given the same sort of ultimatum.

"Sooner or later, my friends, all of you will find yourselves trampled under the cruel heel of the oppressor. The Crescent outfit wants the entire Basin for itself. Brad Leland has boasted that he is building a cattle empire. But at our expense, gentlemen, unless we join together and fight this outright theft of the open range. Now this meeting is open to suggestions . . ."

Pat Olgilvie was feeling the whiskey he'd downed, and with an old man's crankiness said, "Too much palaver. All we need do is ride to Crescent in a body, armed for bear, and run that passel of range-grabbers clear out of the Territory. We could string up a few of them, including that tinhorn Stace Barron, as an object lesson for anybody else that takes a notion to hog the range."

Somebody yelled, "Hear, hear!"

A few men burst into laughter, one calling out, "If you ride up front, Pat, the rest of us will be somewhere behind you when the shooting starts!"

Colonel Mowbrey said sharply, "Order, men. This is no time for levity. Order, please."

When there was quiet again, Will Tolliver rose and said, "Men, I'm just a rancher — and no more of a fighting man than the rest. But we've a man here who's already fought Crescent twice — and lived to tell about it. He aims to go on fighting that outfit, with or without help. He's Ed Jernigan, the mustanger from over in the Brenoso. He's here with us, and I hope he'll now tell us how we can fight and beat Crescent."

Jernigan felt as he might have if dealt a card from the bottom of the deck in a poker game. Being a loner, he couldn't see himself as a leader of men — and certainly he was no speechmaker. But Tolliver sat down, leaving the floor to him, and every pair of eyes in the place looked expectantly his way.

Matt Baylor taunted, "Yeah, Jernigan . . . We'd like to hear from a fast gun like you how Crescent can be licked."

Jernigan thought, *Well, there's no help for it*. He removed his hat, laid it on the table, took the cigar from his mouth, heaved to his feet. For a moment he hadn't a single idea in his head; then suddenly he saw that there was but one way to deal with Crescent.

"Since it's been put up to me," he said, "I say we should ride out there and make that show of strength that Pat mentioned. But we shouldn't go right off with fighting in mind. Barron and his hardcases would fort up, and a lot of us would get shot trying to take them.

"As I see it, we should talk to the outfit's owners — Brad Leland and his brother's widow, Margaret — and make it clear that if Barron and his hardcases move against one of us we'll all move against Crescent — and

85

tear it apart. Then if the Lelands won't back down we should go out there again, armed and provisioned, and lay siege to their headquarters. We could starve the lot of them out and win the fight without bloodshed."

Jernigan paused, wondering if the scheme sounded to the others as though it would work.

He went on, "We'll take Mel Harper along the first time, to show that we want to stay on the right side of the law. That way Crescent can't accuse us of doing other than protecting our rights to the open range. I figure that's the one sensible way to handle the situation."

He sat down, feeling pretty well satisfied.

Colonel Mowbrey said, "It seems a sound idea. Unless somebody has a better one, we'll take a vote as to whether or not we should act on it."

Will Tolliver called out, "Colonel, there can't be any better idea. I move that we all meet at Rincon Monday morning and ride to Crescent in a body."

"Hold on a second," a man at the bar said. "Why waste time making two trips out there? Let's pack along plenty of grub and ammunition and lay siege to that den of side-winders right off. Talking with the Lelands won't gain us a thing. I say we act, not talk, Monday morning."

Another man said, "We'd better not go off half-cocked. Stace Barron is a professional gunfighter, and he's got about twenty hardcases backing him up. He's not likely to let us starve him out. He'll put up a fight, and a lot of us will get our heads blown off."

A third man put in, "I say we should ride out there under cover of darkness — and go in shooting."

Matt Baylor took it up, his voice loud and arrogant enough to command attention. "You hombres are going about it all wrong. If we force a showdown, we'll be playing into that outfit's hands. They'll cut us to pieces, then run those of us left alive clear out of the country — and the whole Basin will be Crescent range. Our only chance is to ruin the Lelands. I can tell you how to do that. I've been thinking on it for a long time."

Baylor had caught the attention of the entire crowd, and knowing it, he stepped out from the bar and took up a stance in the center of the room. His heavy face wore a smug expression, that of a man bending others to his will and finding pleasure in it. Watching him, Jernigan decided that the man sure had plenty of gall. There he was, a stage robber standing up and haranguing a group made up of honest men, and having them hang on his every word. Jernigan knew — felt it — that Baylor would come up with some loco scheme that would throw the meeting into confusion and bring it to a close without anything being decided.

Looking about with an air of self-importance, Baylor went on, "Crescent has more cattle on the range than all the rest of us put together, and those quarter-moon branded critters are just begging to be run off. It we all work at it, we can get away with a couple thousand head before the Lelands and Stace Barron catch on to what's happening. Even when they do catch on, they won't be able to stop their losses. We'll wipe out their herd. We'll turn Crescent into a cattle outfit without a single cow. And I've got it all figured out how we can get those cattle away without any danger to ourselves."

Colonel Mowbrey said disapprovingly, "Rustle Crescent's cattle, Baylor? That would be downright thievery."

Baylor shot back, "That outfit's stealing the range from us, ain't it?"

"It sure is," a man at the bar said. "And stealing range is like stealing money out of a man's pocket — or food out of his mouth."

"Worse still," another man added, "if we try to stop them from stealing it, they kill us."

Yet another called out, "Turn about's fair play . . . Crescent steals our land, and we steal their cattle."

And from one more, angry of voice, "It would sure ruin that outfit — and that's what we want, ain't it?"

With that a dozen or more men began to argue the matter, loudly and heatedly. As Ed Jernigan had known it would be, the meeting was thrown into utter confusion with no hope of anything being decided.

X

Matt Baylor's suggestion finally threw the meeting into an uproar, and Jernigan walked out on it in disgust. Will Tolliver and Pat Olgilvie went with him.

As they rode out of San Miguel, Tolliver said, "It was a good plan, Ed. Too bad things got out of hand. If Matt Baylor had kept his big mouth shut, the others might have followed your lead."

Jernigan shook his head. "I doubt that. If Baylor hadn't come up with his rustling scheme, somebody else would have shot my idea to pieces. There's just no getting a bunch of little ranchers to act together even for their own good. Trouble is, they're all loners at heart — like you and me."

"That's true, I suppose. What will you do now?"

Chuckling, Jernigan said, "I didn't convince that crowd that I know how to fight Crescent, but I did convince myself. I'm riding out there and have a talk with the Lelands."

"Not alone?"

"How else, when I've got no army siding me?"

"You'll get yourself killed, sure."

"I'll run the risk."

"But for what?" Tolliver asked. "What will it gain you?"

"Could be that I can get the Lelands to call off their cross dogs by making them savvy that they've got more to lose than to gain by making war on me."

"If you manage to do that, it won't help the rest of us."

"After what I saw tonight, I'm playing a lone hand and letting everybody else do as they see fit," Jernigan said. "Sorry, Will, but that's how it has to be."

Late the next morning, coming within sight of Crescent Ranch headquarters, Jernigan began to have doubts — to think that maybe he was on a fool's errand. By riding alone into enemy territory, he could end up very dead.

He saw that the Lelands had built big, and solidly. They had, he decided, built for generations of Lelands yet to come.

The bunkhouse, cookshack, barn and numerous sheds stood at one side of a broad yard, the ranchhouse to the other. Each of the sheds was as large as Jernigan's house back at the edge of the Brenoso. As for Crescent's house, it was a huge, two-storied affair with an arched portico across the front.

In the middle of the yard was a roofed, circular-walled well. The crew's cook came from the cookshack with a wooden pail and walked to the well. He gave Jernigan, who was now into the yard, only an incurious glance. Another man, shoeing a horse in one of the sheds, paused at his work and watched him with more interest.

As Jernigan dismounted in front of the house, the door opened and a blonde young woman in a green gingham dress looked at him inquiringly.

"Welcome to Crescent," she said. "Your coming here is a pleasant surprise, for we don't get many visitors."

He took her to be Brad Leland's wife, Kitty. Removing his hat, he said, "Is the other Mrs. Leland at home, ma'am?"

She shook her head. "Nobody's here but me and my father. Margaret is somewhere out on the range. She rides like a man, you know. Or do you know? You seem to know who I am, but I . . . Well, you have the advantage of me." She smiled in friendly fashion. "So I'm not sure if I should ask you to come and wait for her."

"My name is Ed Jernigan, Mrs. Leland."

"Oh, the mustanger."

"Yes, ma'am, I'm that."

She now looked at him with a lively interest, and in a woman's appraising way. She was a rather small woman, quite pretty, and somewhat younger than Margaret Leland. She smiled again, and he detected a mischievous gleam in her eyes.

"Margaret told me all about you, Mr. Jernigan."

He wasn't in a mood to be amused these days, but that brought a grin to his face. "I didn't realize she knew all about me."

"Oh, you made quite an impression on her," Kitty Leland said. "She'll be pleased you've come to call. Do come in, Ed. I may call you that? You just call me 'Kitty' — as everybody does."

"All right, Kitty. But this isn't a social call — or even a friendly one."

"What in the world kind of a call could it be, then?" she asked. And without waiting for an answer, added, "Come on in, you hear?"

He went in, and she led him across a wide hallway into a large, handsomely furnished parlor. This fine, big house made his one-room 'dobe seem grubby indeed. A man gray of hair and moustache sat in an armchair with a drink in one hand and a cigar in the other. He had the flushed, pudgy face of one given to ease and self-indulgence.

Kitty said, "Ed, this is my father, Ben Hazlitt. Daddy, Ed's come to call on Margaret. Isn't that nice?"

Hazlitt nodded, said, "Glad to know you, son. Excuse me for not getting up. My rheumatism is bothering me this morning." He lifted his drink. "A bit of tonic, you understand."

Jernigan said, "Yes, sir. I understand." Remembering what Margaret Leland had told him about this man, he was sure the tonic was straight whiskey. "Glad to know you, Mr. Hazlitt."

"Sit down and make yourself at home, Ed," Kitty said, seating herself on a sofa. She smiled at him brightly. "Margaret rode out hours ago, and so should be home any minute."

Jernigan sat on a straightbacked chair, feeling ill at ease in this house.

Ben Hazlitt said, "So you've come to call on our lovely young widow. I hope, sir, your intentions are honorable."

"As a matter of fact," Jernigan said, "I'm here to talk business."

"Then it's my son-in-law, Brad, you want to see," Hazlitt said. "Or our overseer, Stace Barron. Jernigan . . . ? Haven't I heard that name before?" He stared at Jernigan, suddenly belligerent. "Why, you're one of those no-account ranchers that are giving us so much trouble!"

Kitty again exclaimed, "Father, please!"

At the sound of a horse being ridden into the yard, Kitty said, "That's probably Margaret now." She went to a window, held aside its lace curtain, and looked out. Then: "I'm sorry, Ed . . . It's Brad." She didn't sound sorry. Her voice held a hint of pleasure that told she was a young woman extremely fond of her husband and showed it each time he came riding in.

92

Getting up from his chair, Jernigan said, "I'll talk with him outside."

Brad Leland had dismounted by the well and was now drawing a pail of water. His horse was being led away by the man who had been shoeing the bronc in one of the sheds. Leland was a stocky man in his late twenties. He possessed a boyish sort of good looks. He had pushed his hat back and a curly shock of brown hair had fallen over his brow. He reached for a tin cup that stood on the well wall, filled it from the pail, and then, as he drank, he became aware of Jernigan striding toward him.

Lowering the tin cup, he said in flat, arrogant challenge, "Who are you, mister? What do you want at Crescent?"

"My name's Jernigan — and it should tell you why I'm here."

Leland looked jolted, and burst out, "The hell you say!" He tossed the tin cup into the pail, faced Jernigan with a show of bravado. "You've got a nerve, coming here, but if you're looking for trouble, you won't find it. I'm not armed."

Jernigan had already seen that the man wore no gunrig.

"Could be that a man who hires a gunhand and a bunch of hardcases would figure he has no need to go armed. But he could get himself shot down for having others do his dirty work."

Stung, Leland flushed. He seemed about to make an angry retort, but instead called to the man who had taken his horse.

"You, Charley! Ride out and fetch Stace Barron. You'll find him over by Rock Creek. Tell him there's trouble. Tell him Jernigan's here!" Then, as though fearful Jernigan would try to stop the man, he raised his voice to a shout: "Get moving — fast!"

Charley swung onto the horse, struck out at a hard lope.

Jernigan laughed mockingly. He had Brad Leland's measure now. The man had no backbone. Without his hired gunhand, he was no man at all.

From over by the house, Kitty called, "Brad! Brad, what's wrong?"

Before Leland could reply to that, Ben Hazlitt yelled, "It's all right, Brad. This troublemaker won't pull anything." And his voice sharpening: "Jernigan, I've got a shotgun aimed at you!"

All Jernigan could think at the moment was: *Well, bucko, you've nobody to blame but yourself.*

He swung about to see if Hazlitt really did have a shotgun. The man did. He stood by one of the adobe portico pillars with the weapon cocked and leveled. Brad Leland stepped up behind Jernigan to lift his gun from its holster. He now laughed, in the same mocking way as the mustanger had done.

"Now we'll find out how tough you really are, Jernigan!"

XI

Jernigan had a split second in which to try to save himself. He made use of it, driven by desperation —

94

and by his chagrin over being taken by a boozer on one hand and a weakling on the other.

He made his move as Brad Leland's hand closed on the butt of the gun. Before the man had the revolver clear of its holster, Jernigan grabbed him by the wrist and reeled him off balance with a violent jerk. Holding on to him with his right hand, he spun around and locked his left arm about Leland's neck.

Using him as a shield, he shouted at the man with the shotgun.

"All right, Hazlitt! Go ahead — cut loose with both barrels, if you've a mind to!" Then, as savagely to Leland: "Let go of my gun — quick!"

Leland let the revolver slide back into its holster. Jernigan brought his right hand up and took hold of his left wrist. With this extra leverage, he tightened his hold on the man's neck. Leland began to choke, to strangle.

Jernigan called out, "Kitty, get that shotgun — bring it here!"

Wide-eyed with fright, the young woman turned to her father. Hazlitt hesitated a moment, then eased the shotgun's hammers off cocked position and handed the weapon to her. As she came across the yard, her husband's legs buckled. Jernigan let loose of him and he fell to his hands and knees, gasping agonizingly.

Taking the shotgun from Kitty, Jernigan said, "You've a damn fool for a father. And another for a husband, the truth be told."

She stared at him with furious, hating eyes, and said, her voice off-key, "You awful man, you!" She bent over her husband, murmuring to him as to a hurt child.

95

A rhythmic drumming of hooves turned Jernigan about toward the rider coming in at a lope. This time it was Margaret Leland.

His anger subsided somewhat as he watched her come into the yard. A pretty sight, he had to admit. An attractive young woman on a fine buckskin horse. No side-saddle for her. She rode astride, and handled a mount as expertly as most men. She wore a divided skirt, boots, a mannish blouse, a broad-brimmed, flat-crowned hat. He was so taken by her that he all but forgot the other people there.

Margaret's amber-flecked brown eyes took in the scene here, even before she reined in, and, seeming to know exactly what had happened, she let anger show on her face.

Dismounting, she said, "I'm sorry I wasn't here when you came, Ed. This wouldn't have taken place if I had been." She glanced at Brad Leland, who was now getting to his feet with Kitty's help. "Can't a person even visit Crescent without being brutalized?" she demanded of him, her voice abrasive.

She received no reply, only a sullen look from Leland.

His wife said, "Don't be cross with him, Margaret. Can't you see he's been hurt?" Then, to her husband: "Come along, darling . . . Come into the house and lie down."

"Not yet," Jernigan said. "Not until he's heard what I came here to say." He divided a look between Leland and Margaret, hardening his heart against the latter too. "Since you two are the owners of this outfit, I'm

96

serving notice on you that I've had a bellyful of Crescent's high and mighty ways. My idea in coming here was to tell you what you may not know — that Stace Barron and his toughhands are making war on me. Barron himself shot eight of my horses. He had three of his men beat my hired hand, a harmless old man, almost to death. He tore down my fence and threw cattle onto my range. He's got some of his hardcases squatting in my ranchhouse. Now you know what that hired gunhand of yours is pulling, if you didn't before, and why I came here."

Margaret again turned her angry gaze on Brad Leland. "Did you know about this?"

"All I know is that Crescent needs all the range it can get," he said sullenly. "If Stace thinks we need this mustanger's range, then he's got to clear out — like the rest of the riffraff around here."

Looking back at Jernigan, Margaret said, "You'll have to accept my word that I didn't know about it. But even if I had known I couldn't have stopped it. Even though I am one of the owners of this outfit, I have no say in its operation. Neither does Brad, actually. Barron does as he pleases."

She was silent for a moment, biting down on her lower lip — looking distressed.

"This isn't happening because Crescent needs your range," she went on. "It's because of what happened in Rincon that day. And that was because of me. If I hadn't asked to talk with you, gone to that restaurant with you . . ." She shook her head against the wrongness of it. "Don't try to fight him, Ed. It will cost you your life. Crescent will pay you damages . . . for the horses you lost, and for your buildings. I'll see that you're given something for your hired hand, even though money can't possibly make up for the hurt and indignity he suffered. Then you must go away, Ed — far away. To be safe."

Before Jernigan could say that he wouldn't run, Brad Leland took it up.

"We're not paying him a red cent," he said. "No grubby mustanger can come here and demand money of Crescent."

Surprisingly, Kitty said, "It's only fair, Brad. If Stace Barron did such awful things to him, we should make it up to him."

"We have only his word for it."

"I believe him," Kitty said. "And so do you. Because you know what Stace is like."

Some of his bluster gone, Leland said, "All right, we'll pay him. We'll pay him for his buildings too, because we're keeping his range. The usual two hundred dollars, though — not a cent more."

From over by the house Ben Hazlitt called, "Here comes Stace now. He'll settle this thing — his way."

And Brad Leland, with a return of his bravado, said, "Now we'll see just how tough you are, mustanger!" He sounded jubilant.

Jernigan saw that Barron was riding in with only the man who had been sent to fetch him. He was surprised, having expected the gunhand to bring along some of his hardcases to side him. He disposed of the shotgun, feeling sure that Barron wouldn't give him the chance to bring it into play if there was shooting. He preferred to put his trust in his handgun. Removing the loads from the shotgun, he leaned it against the well wall. He noticed that Margaret made a point of moving to his side as the two riders came into the yard.

He had a hunch there wouldn't be any shooting, and shaking his head, said, "I'm obliged to you, but it's not necessary that you stand between him and me. He won't force a fight."

She looked at him wonderingly. "What makes you so sure?"

"His kind always needs the edge," he told her. "And he hasn't brought it with him."

Margaret looked not at all reassured.

The ranchhand, Charley, pulled up by the corral. He dismounted and began off-saddling his mount, as though to show that having fetched Barron he was now out of it. He wore no gunrig, Jernigan noted.

Barron slow-walked his big black horse to the center of the yard. He remained in the saddle after reining in. His dark face was expressionless, but his pale eyes touched Jernigan with anger and hatred.

"If you've got any complaints, make them to me — not to these people," he said. "And if you make them to me, you'll be wasting your breath."

"I figured that," Jernigan told him. "That's why I made them to the Lelands. But I'll say this to you, gunhand . . . You've got until sundown today to move your men and cattle out of my valley. If you don't move them, I will."

"That's open range, mustanger. You can't lay claim to it. That fence you built was illegal."

"By sundown today," Jernigan said and, turning abruptly, he strode to his horse.

Mounting the dun, Jernigan swung it toward the four people by the well. He gave each of them a long, hard look, Margaret last of all.

"You're boxed in here, I can see," he told her. "It's a sorry thing for anybody, and especially a woman like you, to be caught in such a trap."

Barron said, "You're wasting your breath, just like I said you would be, mustanger. When this outfit gets to be what I aim to make it, she'll understand that I did it as much for her as for Brad. Now *adiós* to you, Jernigan." His tone was not just mocking, but contemptuous as well. "You've nowhere to go, but take yourself there anyway."

Jernigan still looked at Margaret, ignoring the gunhand. "Forty dollars for each of those eight horses would be fair damages. If you're still of a mind to pay for them, you can leave the money with the stage company agent at Rincon. If you want to do something for my hired hand, his name is Miguel Rojas and he's laid up at the house of señora Gomez in the Mexican part of Rincon."

Now he looked at Barron. "That's a matter you and I have to settle, your having that old man beaten. It will be at a time and place of my choosing."

"You won't last that long, mustanger," Barron retorted. "I once told you that you're a dead man — and that still holds."

Margaret said, "I'll leave the money with the agent — and see your hired hand too."

Jernigan nodded and as he walked the dun away from Crescent headquarters he felt that his back was as big a target as the side of a barn.

When out on the range, he lifted his mount to a lope and headed for Rincon. He rode into the town shortly before noon and went to the Welcome Café for dinner. After his meal, he rode to the Star Livery Stable, where he bought a roan gelding and a packsaddle for it. With the new horse in tow, he went to Barton's Mercantile, to buy a stock of provisions. After stowing his purchases in the *aparejos* of the packsaddle, he rode around to the Mexican quarter. He found Miguel Rojas sitting in the shade outside señora Gomez's house.

"*Como 'stá, amigo?*"

"I am healing. How goes it with you, Ed?"

"I'm still alive and kicking," Jernigan told him, dismounting.

He hunkered down by the old-timer, who looked somewhat recovered from the beating but far from his usual self.

Rolling a smoke and then handing the makings to Miguel, Jernigan told him what had happened at Slash J Ranch."

"So I don't have a roof over my head," he ended up. "As you can see, I've outfitted for a stay in the *malpais*."

Miguel looked troubled. "You can't win a fight against such odds, Ed. No man could."

"A man can't be run out of his home and not fight, either. Not my kind, anyway."

"If I felt even a little better, I would go with you."

"I know you would, *compadre*."

They were silent for a time, lost in gloomy thought.

Finally Miguel said, "In this kind of a fight, a man can win only by killing the *jefe* of those against him."

Jernigan nodded. "But the time has got to be right for that. And the place. If the showdown isn't of my choosing, Barron will do for me. He's a gunhand by trade, remember."

"*Sí*. You will have to be careful — and lucky."

"I'll be careful," Jernigan said. "And I figure on making my own luck."

When leaving Rincon, he headed northeast across the Basin and late in the afternoon entered the Brenoso Badlands at a point far north of his valley. After some searching, he found water, a small creek in a narrow canyon, and set up camp by it.

He lay wakeful, watching the stars appear in the darkening patch of sky above the canyon walls. He felt utterly alone in the world — and infinitely lonely. He realized that his low spirits came of his being homeless as well as from his having such great odds to fight. Fight he would, but he could win only by killing Stace Barron.

He thought of Margaret Leland, and he knew that when he went up against Barron it would be for her as well as for himself. In a way, Margaret was even worse off than himself. She was caught in a trap, while he remained free and could fight back.

102

He slept finally, but at midnight crawled from his blankets, pulled on his boots, donned his gunrig and hat. He saddled his dun horse and, mounting it, rode out of the canyon. He picked his way through the dark hills in the direction of his valley.

Two hours later he climbed a slope on foot, carrying his rifle, and looked down on his buildings. Tonight the moon hung in a cloudless sky, and in its light he made out the squat shapes of the house and barn. After peering steadily for a few minutes he saw horses in the corral by the barn. The men down there had recovered their mounts, then. Or somebody from Crescent had caught them up and returned them.

The possibility that Barron had reinforced the three men occurred to Jernigan. But he decided that Barron, being an extremely vain man, would play a hand as he'd dealt it for himself. Therefore those three were most likely still on their own.

Three or more, it didn't matter. He was going to give Crescent another fight.

On the chance that the men below were still keeping a night watch, he worked his way stealthily down into the valley.

Finally, when within easy pistol shot of the house, he circled about in the same cautious manner to the rear of the barn. He neither saw nor heard anybody doing sentry duty. He eased up to the barn and worked his way along the rear of it, then around its corner and along its side. At the front corner he paused and studied the house a hundred feet away.

He could see that the door of the house was shut, and the moonlight was bright enough to show him that no one watched from the windows — either from the intact one or the one with the bullet-shattered panes.

He slipped around the corner, moved to the wide doorway of the barn. He had taken a single step inside when a voice from the deep darkness there caused him to start violently — and to utter a grunt of alarm. He had blundered into the building without giving a thought to the possibility that one of the Crescent men would be bedded down in it . . . On the chance that if he, Ed Jernigan, showed up they could again try to catch him in a crossfire.

XII

Jernigan peered this way and that, trying to spot the Crescent hand in the black darkness.

He hadn't caught the first words spoken, only the sound of the half-awake voice. Now he heard the man say, in clear alarm, "Tex — Harry, that you? Talk up, why don't you?"

Mumbling the words, Jernigan said, "It's me — Harry."

"Well, what's up, you big stupe?"

Moving toward the man's voice, Jernigan said, "Something woke me up. I just wanted to make sure you're all right."

The Crescent hand burst out with an oath, yelled, "You ain't Harry!" and reared to his feet.

104

Jernigan saw him as an obscure shape in the gloom.

"Easy now," he said. "Just take it easy — or you're a dead man."

"The mustanger, by damn!"

"That's right — the mustanger. So you'll just drop your gun, if you have the sense of a jughead mule."

Jernigan discovered that the Crescent hand had no sense at all. The man had come to his feet without his gun and now leaned down to pick it up. By the time he came erect again, with the weapon in his hand, Jernigan had him beaded.

"Don't try it! You haven't a chance!"

He could have saved his breath. That same instant the barn seemed to rock with the blast of the man's gun. He had fired with frantic haste, and so missed his mark. But Jernigan couldn't count on him missing again, and so gave him no further chance to save himself. His rifle spurted powderflame, and the Crescent hand, hit, reeled backward under the impact of the slug.

Jernigan had another shot ready, but stayed his finger in the Winchester's trigger. As he had thought, a second slug wasn't needed. The hit man slid down the wall and lay in a crumpled heap, afterward not moving again.

Jernigan swung around and took up a position to one side of the doorway. He would have thought the shooting loud enough to wake the dead, but he saw no signs that the other Crescent men had been roused from sleep.

They're awake . . . Just playing it cagey.

Not a patient man, Jernigan had to force himself to stay in the barn and keep watch on the house. Long minutes passed — at least ten minutes, he guessed — before anything happened.

Then across the yard the door swung open. No one appeared but a man called out, "Jernigan?" His voice was edgy, worried — maybe frightened. "You, Jernigan . . . we know you're there!"

Jernigan remained mouse-quiet, figuring that the longer the others were unsure of his whereabouts the greater his advantage. Sooner or later one or more might come outside. There were but two of them, he believed — since the man he'd shot here in the barn had mentioned only two names. As he'd figured, Barron had not brought in reinforcements.

One at the door, but keeping out of sight. And the other?

Jernigan thought he knew about the other. There was a back door, and the second man had left the house by it. He would be at one side or the other of the 'dobe, hoping his partner could get him, Jernigan, to give his whereabouts away, so he could get a shot at him. Tricky, these Crescent hands. But they kept using the same trick over and over, that of trying to catch him in a crossfire.

The man in the house called out again, uneasiness still in his voice, "We know you're there, mustanger. You haven't a chance. So throw your guns out and come out with your hands up — and we'll let you go your way. What do you say, mustanger? That's fair, ain't it?"

106

The barn had no windows, and no rear door — worse luck. Jernigan would have to stay where he was, in spite of his lack of patience. He couldn't withdraw and try to outflank the pair.

He kept watching the doorway yonder, and each front corner of the house. Neither of the Crescent men showed himself. His patience running out finally, he backed away from the doorway and leaned his rifle against the adobe wall. He went to the small stack of sacked grain, which he had lain in for his horses — when he still had some horses, he thought sourly. He heaved a sack of oats onto his right shoulder and returned to the side of the doorway.

He called out, "You over there, I'm coming out — but I'm coming shooting!"

He heaved the sack of oats off his shoulder and through the doorway, then grabbed up his rifle. As he had hoped, shots blasted before the sack hit the ground. A flurry of shots. Two guns firing.

The edgy voice yelled, "Tex, he's down! We got him!"

Another voice said warily, "Something's down, but I don't know . . . It's too dark over there to tell. We'd better go easy."

More shots racketed, and now Jernigan saw that one of the guns blazing away at the sack of oats was at the side of the house to his right. He would expose less of himself by shooting at the man there than at the one in the doorway. He fired three fast shots at the spot where that one's gun had spurted powderflame. With the third shot, there was an outcry from the Crescent man and he reeled like a drunk away from the side of the house.

After taking three lurching steps, he collapsed to the ground.

"Tex, you hit? Tex . . . ?"

Panic was in the voice of the man within the house, and then he, like his gun, was silent.

The downed man made no movement, uttered no sound, and Jernigan decided he was dead. He waited, watching only the doorway now. The panicky man inside did not show himself, didn't risk exposing himself to shoot again.

Some minutes passed, and then: "Jernigan, listen . . . I'll give up. I'll throw out my gun — my rifle too. You give me your word you'll let me go?"

Jernigan's tension eased, but now anger took hold of him. An anger for the senselessness of it all, for his having had to kill those two men to reclaim his buildings.

"You over there, what's your name?"

"Harry — Harry Bates." Then, with a feeble anger of his own, Bates said, "You're a holy terror, Jernigan. You've done for all three of the boys who were with me."

"Boys, hell," Jernigan shot back. "They were no-good hardcases hired for fighting wages to make war on a lot of poor, dumb two-bit ranchers. And you're another, Harry Bates!"

"You're going to kill me?"

"Why should I let you go — to make a try at me another day?"

"I won't, I swear," Bates said, whining now. "I've a bellyful of fighting you. I'll ride clear out of this

108

country, if you'll just give me the chance. Here . . . I'm throwing out my guns."

Jernigan heard some object that could have been a gun fall into the middle of the yard. A moment later he heard something else land there, maybe a rifle.

Then, from Harry Bates: "You can't kill a man in cold blood, friend. You just can't!"

Friend, Jernigan thought disgustedly.

He said, "All right, *friend* . . . . That's what you'll do. You'll ride clear out of this country. After you've dug a couple of graves and buried your partners. Now I'll tell you what to do right off . . . Light the lamp over there."

With the blooming of lamplight, Jernigan moved out into the yard and across it to the house. Harry Bates stood in the middle of the room, his empty hands raised. He was a big man, tall and heavy-boned but spare of flesh. His face was angular, rough-hewn. Hardcase he might be, but only when he had plenty of his own kind siding him. Now, very much alone, he didn't even assume a pose of bravado. The mustanger saw fear in his eyes and sensed that he was about to plead for his life again.

"Only about an hour until dawn," Jernigan said. "No use you going back to bed. Get a fire started and breakfast on. We've a busy day ahead of us."

"Busy? What do you mean by that?"

"You'll see," Jernigan told him. "Just hop to it now."

After they had eaten, he saw to it that the Crescent man washed up the breakfast things and then tidied up the 'dobe.

With the first light of dawn, he selected a site for the graves, a spot well away from the buildings, and put the Crescent man to work with a shovel. While Bates was opening the earth, Jernigan gathered together the hardcases' firearms and disposed of them in the creek.

Leaving Bates to fill in the graves, Jernigan went to the corral to rope and saddle one of the horses. He left it by the creek, to drink and graze, then entered the barn and began digging out the pair of saddlebags he had hidden there which contained his savings of twenty-two hundred dollars. He placed them and his rifle on the horse's saddle. Mounting, he rode to the corral and drove the other Crescent animals from it.

He drove those three out of the valley, afterward swinging north through the hills to where he had left his own dun horse. He transferred his saddlebags, his rifle and himself to the dun, and with the Crescent horse in tow, returned to the valley. He dismounted at the creek, to let the dun drink. Bates was still working at the graves, taking his own good time, and Jernigan had a smoke while waiting for him to finish the job.

Finally the Crescent man returned the shovel to the barn.

Coming over to Jernigan, he said, "What now?"

"Now we'll move those cattle out of the valley, friend," Jernigan told him, again giving the word "friend" a sour emphasis.

Riding together, they gathered the Crescent cattle — nearly sixty head — and drove them out onto the Basin range. By that time half the morning was gone, and

Jernigan dismounted to rest his horse and have a smoke.

Looking at him uncertainly, Bates asked, "Can I light out now?"

"Not yet," Jernigan said while spilling tobacco from sack to paper. "Get down and take it easy for a spell. You've a long ride ahead of you yet today. Just keep your distance, though. I wouldn't want to have to kill you for trying to jump me."

"No need for you to worry I'll pull anything," Bates said sullenly. "I know when not to crowd my luck."

He dismounted and leaned dejectedly against a boulder about twenty feet from where the mustanger was hunkered down with his back to another rock.

Puffing on his cigarette, Jernigan gave him a long, speculative look. Here was a big man, a rough, tough man, a man who was certainly dangerous when the odds were in his favor. At other times, he was short on guts — not much more of a man than, say, Brad Leland. Most of the hardcased breed were shaped in that mold, Jernigan told himself. And even when the odds gave them plenty of nerve, they weren't any great shakes as fighters. He began to take hope that he still might win out over the Crescent outfit — which was, of course, Stace Barron.

"How many hombres like you at Crescent, Harry?"

Bates gave him a surprised look, for his tone had changed from hostile to neutral. The man also appeared to experience a sense of relief, as though only now becoming convinced that the mustanger wouldn't kill him in the end.

"Stace brought in eighteen of us," Bates said. "He kept on only four of the old Crescent hands."

"So with three men killed and you on your way out of the country only fourteen are left."

"Yeah. That's the size of it."

"What's Barron's hold on Brad Leland?"

Bates shook his head. "He never said. Stace is close-mouthed."

"But he does have a hold on Leland — right?"

"I figure so," Bates said. "Stace has to have one, else he couldn't have taken the outfit over like he's done. What's this long ride I've got to make, Jernigan?"

"What you said," Jernigan told him. "A ride clear out of this country. We'll get started on it shortly."

"We?"

"I'm going to see you on your way, Harry," Jernigan said. Then, grinning: "That's mighty friendly of me, wouldn't you say?"

XIII

Three of them this time, two horseback and one driving a wagon.

Jernigan let them get almost to his buildings, then rode down to swing in behind them.

This was late in the morning of the second day after he had left Harry Bates on the stage road. He had set up his hideaway camp in the canyon again and come here to see if Barron had moved more men into his

112

valley. These three had appeared soon after he took up a watching position in the hills.

The two mounted men were not yet aware of him. They lifted their horses to a lope, rode into the ranchyard. They remained in their saddles, and he could imagine their puzzling over the absence of the four men who were supposed to be holding down the place.

The driver of the rig was aware of him. This man looked back over his shoulder a couple of times. Strangely enough, he didn't call out a warning to the riders. Jernigan recognized him from the day he had gone to Crescent headquarters. Charley, the hand Brad Leland had sent to fetch Stace Barron.

Jernigan swung alongside the rig, noting first that Charley again was not armed and then that the wagon was loaded with provisions. It also carried, he saw, a couple of blanket rolls and war sacks.

He said, "Friend, you might as well turn back with that stuff. Those four Crescent hands won't be needing more grub — and these two won't be staying."

Charley reined in his team. "Dead, the other four?"

"Three are. The other left for a healthier climate."

Charley was a man of sixty or more. His face was weathered to old leather. Grinning, he said, "Mustanger, you're a real hellion. But watch out for those two yonder. They're tough hombres. Barron sent them to move in with the others — to make things harder for you. But even alone they can be as deadly as sidewinders."

"I'll have to find that out for myself," Jernigan said.

The two in the ranchyard had seen him now. After some debate they came slow-walking their horses out from the buildings.

He swung his dun away from the rig and dismounted with his rifle. They reined in fifty feet from him, one a Mexican with a badly pockmarked face and the other having a scar running across his left cheek from mouth to ear. The mustanger felt an immediate thrust of anger at sight of that scarred face. This one, he knew, he would be able to kill without experiencing a single twinge of conscience afterward.

Scar-face said, "You're Jernigan, are you?"

"I am. And you're one of the hombres who gave my hired hand that beating."

"On orders," Scar-face said. "If that's sticking in your craw, take it up with Stace Barron. What happened to the hands he sent out here?"

"Three are in their graves, and one long gone."

"You saying you killed three of them and drove the fourth man off?"

"I'm saying it," Jernigan said. "Now you and your *amigo* make your play — or get rid of your guns."

Scar-face either liked the odds of two to one or was made of sterner stuff than Harry Bates. He kept sizing Jernigan up, his right hand resting on his thigh within inches of his holstered gun. His gaze was steady, and a faint, contemptuous smile curled his thin lips. Because of his ugly scar, it was a sinister smile. He was going to make a play, and Jernigan found himself quite willing to have it so — for old Miguel.

114

"Manuel, you move off a little," Scar-face said. "Give me room to call this mustanger's bluff."

The Mexican said uneasily, "Listen, Jake . . . Don't start a fight."

"Move off, I tell you. Give me room."

It wasn't room Jake needed. He was hoping that with the two of them separated Jernigan would have to shift his gaze back and forth between them. That would give him a chance to make his play without too much risk to himself. One thing was clear to the mustanger: this man considered himself a fast gun and also had plenty of nerve. The thing to do, Jernigan decided, was to ignore Manuel for the time being and keep his gaze steady on Jake.

The Mexican reined his horse away from beside Jake's mount, rode off about ten yards. Jernigan watched Jake fixedly, ready to go into action with his rifle.

Then, from Charley: "Watch the Mex, Jernigan. He's the dangerous one."

The warning came just in time for Jernigan to save himself. Throwing a look at Manuel, he saw him already in the act of drawing. He flung himself to the ground, as he had intended to do when Jake drew, and brought his rifle into firing position. Manuel's gun blasted, but his aim was spoiled by Jernigan's maneuver. Before he could fire again, the mustanger drove a shot at him — the range so short for a rifle he couldn't have missed — and he so sure of his aim he didn't wait to see that the Mexican was hit. He reared up to one foot and one knee, lined his sights on Jake.

The scar-faced hardcase had his gun out and was steadying it for a shot. He fired an instant too late, for Jernigan got off his shot and hit him as he squeezed the trigger. The Winchester's slug caught Jake dead-center in the chest. He spilled loosely from the saddle and hit the ground face-down, then abruptly became still.

Jernigan threw another load into his rifle, swung the weapon to bead the Mexican again. Manuel was slumped forward in the saddle, his gun dropped to the ground and his left hand pressing against his right shoulder. Blood was seeping between his fingers, and spreading in a widening crimson stain over his shirt. He kneed his horse into motion, started away.

"You there, hombre," Jernigan called out. "You're not going anywhere. Get off that bronc, or I'll shoot you off."

Manuel looked at him with pain-filled eyes, reined his horse in and eased himself from its back. He sank to the ground, sat crosslegged, holding his left hand to his wound.

Jernigan thought with bitter satisfaction: *Six down, twelve to go — and then Stace Barron.*

He looked at the Crescent man on the wagon. "Thanks. You saved my hide, sure."

"I've a bellyful of that crowd," Charley said. "The more of them you do away with the better I'll like it. I worked for Steve Leland and his father before him, and I can't stomach what's happening to the outfit they built up."

"You want to haul this dead one back to Crescent?"

116

"Sure. It'll be something to see Barron's face when he has a look at the body — and hears what happened to the rest of the toughhands he sent out here."

"What about that one?" Charley asked, nodding toward Manuel.

"I'll get rid of him," Jernigan said. "If you don't know how I do it, Barron can't make you tell him."

"I almost forgot," Charley said, taking a folded paper from his shirt pocket. "Mrs. Leland slipped this here message to me just before we pulled out. She said I was to give it to you if I happened to see you and got the chance."

Wonderingly, Jernigan took the paper. "*Gracias,*" he said, and unfolded it as Charley drove away.

The message was a brief note written in a small, neat hand.

Ed: I'm hoping against hope that by some miracle this will reach you. I must see you, to warn you of how S. B. is planning to trap you. I'll be in Rincon, at the Territorial House, tomorrow night. Please come if you can. Margaret.

He read the few lines a second and then a third time, feeling somehow good about the message. He hardly needed a warning that Stace Barron was planning to trap him, but he would of course see Margaret. Ed Jernigan wasn't, he reflected, a man to turn down a chance to be with a pretty woman.

He folded the note, tucked it into his shirt pocket, then turned to the wounded Mexican.

117

"On your feet, hombre," he said. "We'll go into the house. I'll patch you up as best I can; then you and I will take a trip across the *malpais*."

He had just finished cleansing and bandaging the Crescent man's wound when he heard a rider approaching. As he picked up his rifle and turned to the door, the rider called his name.

It was Will Tolliver. He had reined in at the edge of the yard.

"Come on in," Jernigan told him. "It's safe enough — for the moment."

Tolliver came forward and dismounted. "I was out doing some scouting, trying to find out what had happened to you, Ed. I was worried, not having heard from you. Then I met Charley Faraday, and he told me you were here — safe and sound. Where's the Mex you shot?"

"Inside. Come on in."

Manuel was seated at the plank table, a study in dejection. He had his hat and shirt off, and he was heavily bandaged about his right shoulder with the arm in a sling. He had suffered a nasty wound, and needed more than flour-sack dressings on it. He would be a long time in using his right arm, in handling a gun, and Jernigan had given up his plan to take him across the Brenoso and send him down the stage trail, as he had done with Harry Bates.

"You need a doctor, hombre," the mustanger told him. "Can you make it to Rincon, do you think?"

"There is a man at San Miguel who can fix a bullet wound. I can make it that far."

118

Jernigan handed him his hat.

"I can go, then?" Manuel said uncertainly.

"I sure don't want you for a boarder."

Manuel went to the door, faced about there. *"Muchas gracias,"* he said, and stepped outside.

Tolliver and Jernigan watched the Mexican mount up, and ride away at a slow walk; then the mustanger told Tolliver, "I'm not here to stay." With a wry grin, he added, "I don't aim to commit suicide. I've a hideout camp back in the hills, and I'll hole up there until I know what my next move is to be. Anything new with you Basin ranchers, Will?"

"We had another meeting last night at San Miguel. Not all of the boys showed up. Matt Baylor took over the proceedings and argued for riding to Crescent in the middle of the night and taking that crowd by surprise. Nothing came of it."

"He's quit talking about running off Crescent's cattle?"

"Not at all. He figures the cattle can be taken any time after Stace Barron, Brad Leland and their toughhands have been run off the range — or killed. Why he's changed his tune, I don't know. Somehow, I no longer trust that hombre."

"I can tell you about Matt Baylor," Jernigan said. "He's not to be trusted any farther than a man could throw him. He was one of the hombres who held up that stage, Will."

"Why didn't you let it be known, for Pete's sake?"

Jernigan shook his head, showing he regretted not having let that be known. "It was dumb of me. But I didn't know until the night we attended the meeting that he lived in the Basin. And I didn't go to the law about him earlier because — well, you know what kind of a lawman Mel Harper is. When I saw him at the meeting, putting up a show of being an honest rancher, I knew it would do no good to brand him a road agent at that late date. It would have been my word against his — and most of the Basin men knew him better than they did me."

"Since he's that sort, he can't have the interest of the rest of us in mind when he talks of raiding Crescent."

"Could be he figures that if the little ranchers manage to run off the Crescent people he can grab all or most of the outfit's cattle for himself. Maybe he even hopes to take over Crescent headquarters — and live in high style."

Tolliver nodded. "He must be hoping to come out ahead of the game. I'll spread the word around that he's not to be trusted."

After a little more talk, they left the house and mounted their horses.

"I'm heading into the hills, Will," Jernigan said. "See you around."

"Take care, Ed," Tolliver told him.

Late the following afternoon, Jernigan rode from his hideout camp and headed for Rincon to keep his rendezvous with Margaret Leland. He timed himself to arrive there after nightfall, and even undercover of darkness did not risk riding into the town. He was learning caution if not patience. There might be

Crescent hands in town, more of them than he could take on.

He left his horse in a brush thicket off to the side of the place and walked through the darkness to the rear of the two-storied Territorial House.

Entering the hotel by the back door, he walked down the hallway to the lobby. Hiram Walther, the immensely fat proprietor, sat at the table in the center of the room with another townsman. The two were playing dominoes, and Walther looked up with a frown of annoyance at having the game interrupted.

"Oh, it's you, Jernigan . . . Why the back door?"

"I don't know that the street is safe for me. Did you notice any Crescent riders in town tonight?"

"I didn't see any. Did you, Al?"

The other domino-player said, "I saw some horses in the quarter-moon brand at the Longhorn Saloon's hitch-rack."

Jernigan thought: *So I was right in taking care.* He was aware of a sudden uneasiness in him. It was a feeling that all was not right. A hunch that he shouldn't have come to town.

Always nosy, Walther said, "There's been talk about that outfit gunning for you, Jernigan. They're still after you, eh?"

"They're still after me. Which room is Mrs. Leland in?"

"Mrs. Leland? Why, man, neither of those ladies is a guest here right now. Which Mrs. Leland were you expecting to see? Probably the widow, eh?"

"Yeah, the widow," Jernigan said, his uneasiness growing. "You're sure she's not here?"

"Take a look at the register, if you don't believe me."

Jernigan went to the desk, turned the book around. Margaret's name wasn't there. His uneasiness became suspicion-tinged alarm. He looked back over the signature until he found Margaret's for the night she had stayed here after the stage holdup. Then he took the note from his pocket and compared its handwriting with that of her signature. The two did not match at all. The writing of the note was small and neat, that in the book bold and mannish rather than feminine. Margaret hadn't written the note.

Jernigan swore under his breath, angry as well as alarmed. He had been tricked, hoodwinked. Charley had said that Mrs. Leland had given him the note to deliver, but he hadn't said which Mrs. Leland. It had been Mrs. Brad Leland — not Mrs. Margaret Leland.

Margaret had nothing to do with it. It was Kitty. Stace Barron — and maybe her husband — got her to write it. To bait me into a trap.

This meant, Jernigan realized, that Barron had discovered that he had gotten rid of the four Crescent hands at his ranch. It meant that the gunhand had sent Jake and Manuel, along with the wagonload of provisions, to bait him into making a play. Barron had hoped the two hardcases would manage to kill him, but had the note Charley carried as a hole card if the pair failed in that. They had failed, but the note had served its purpose. Or almost had. If he had ridden into

Rincon, the trap Barron had set for him tonight would have sprung. If he hadn't come in on foot, by the back way, he would almost certainly be dead now.

Hiram Walther said, "What ails you, Jernigan? You look as though you've been mule-kicked."

Jernigan shook his head, and said, not to the hotelman but to himself, "I've got to get out of here."

He went across the lobby to go down the hallway and out the back door. A voice stopped him, caused him to spin about with his hand on his gun.

The voice said, in sharp warning: "Not that way, bucko. They've already spotted you in here — and a pair of them is out back, waiting to shoot you full of holes."

Jernigan stared with mingled disbelief and distrust, for the owner of the voice was Matt Baylor.

XIV

Jernigan's alarm over having blundered into a trap was tempered by the confused feelings touched off in him by Matt Baylor.

Curious as well as suspicious, he said, "Why, Baylor? What's your game — warning me like this when I'm the man who killed your brother?"

Baylor stepped into the lobby, kicked the door shut. He struck a cocky pose, his thumbs hooked in his cartridge-studded gunbelt. His broad, tough face wore a bemused grin, but his eyes mirrored something else. Hatred, certainly, Jernigan thought.

"Why, I'll tell you, bucko," the burly man said. "I have a friend at Crescent who keeps me posted. I heard from him about Barron setting this trap for you. And I heard from him how you've been doing away with that gunslick's hardcases. I want you to stay alive to do away with more of them. When you have that crew cut down to a size that I can handle, I'll make my move against that range-grabbing outfit."

He paused, and when he spoke again his grin was replaced by a scowl.

"As for your killing Chuck, I haven't forgotten it — not for a second. I'll settle with you for that, hombre, when I've no more use for you."

"All right," Jernigan said. "Right now I'd take the Devil himself for a partner. Barron's got men laying for me out front too, hasn't he?"

"He sure has," Baylor said, his grin returning. "A couple friends of yours — Russ Kiley and that kid, Tobie. One's in the doorway of the saddle shop across the street, the other in the alleyway there."

"What about Barron himself?"

"He's standing in front of the Alhambra Saloon, smoking a cigar and waiting to nail you if his toughhands don't."

"So how do I get out of this gun-trap?"

"By my siding you," Baylor said. "We go out shooting, you and me. I'll take the Tobie kid in the alleyway and you Kiley in the doorway."

Jernigan gave that a moment of hard thought, decided there was no other way he could get out of the trap alive.

"All right," he said. "If we manage to take those two, you cover me so the pair around back don't come running and jump me — and I'll go after Barron. Agreed?"

Baylor nodded. "It's agreed. Now you, fat man, put out that lamp. We can't have a light behind us when we go out of here."

Hiram Walther and his fellow townsman had become edgy while listening to the conversation. Now the hotelman heaved his massive self to his feet, pulled down the hanging lamp. He turned the wick low, then blew into the chimney and extinguished the flame.

With the lobby plunged into darkness, Baylor yelled, "Come on, Jernigan — come on!"

Jernigan would have known now if he hadn't before that Matt Baylor was a wild one. Drawing his gun, he moved through the gloom and was just behind the burly man when he opened the door and leaped out onto the hotel porch. Putting his trust wholly in Baylor, he fixed his gaze on the doorway of the saddle shop. Before he could make out if there was a man there, violence erupted.

Matt Baylor bellowed, "Here's Jernigan, you no-good Crescent sons — and I'm siding him!"

A shouted voice lifted across the street: "Watch it, Tobie — watch it!"

That was surely Kiley, Jernigan thought — and brought his gun to bear on the obscure figure in the doorway.

Both men over there opened fire, as did Baylor. The muzzle flashes of the guns were bright against the darkness. The heavy blasts of the Colt's .45's seemed thunderous. Jernigan heard the shriek of a slug passing so close he couldn't doubt that the shot had been aimed at him. He wished for his rifle, since the range was long for a handgun. Lacking it, he went down the porch steps, jumped the plank sidewalk, dropped to his knees and his left hand. Another slug whipped past him. He drove one shot and then another at the man in the doorway. At *him* and into him.

Russ Kiley came staggering out of the saddle shop doorway, cursing Ed Jernigan and getting off one more shot before collapsing.

Baylor and Tobie were making a duel of it, and Jernigan, picking himself up, started along the street at a run. He was after Stace Barron now, the man he really wanted — needed — to catch in his sights. He could see the gunhand move out from in front of the Alhambra Saloon and jerk a rifle from his horse's saddle at the hitchrack.

Jernigan pulled up short, looking for cover. The rifle gave Barron the edge his kind always needed. A Concord coach with its wheels removed stood on low wooden blocks outside the stage company's stables. Jernigan darted for it just as Barron got off a shot. He crouched in the narrow space between the coach and the stable wall, and waited for the gunhand to come closer. His heart was hammering again, and his breathing was labored.

Barron yelled tauntingly, "What's the matter, mustanger? You wanted a showdown with me — so come and have it. You lost your nerve?"

He didn't come any closer, but began shooting as fast as he could work his rifle's lever and trigger. Unable to see Jernigan, he was hoping to hit him with a blind, heavy fire. To Jernigan it sounded as though the gunhand's slugs were tearing the coach apart. Wood splinters pelted him.

Behind him the racketing of guns had ceased, and Matt Baylor's jubilant yell rang out: "I've downed the kid, mustanger! Another of those sons done for!"

He'd no sooner gotten the words out then another flurry of shots crashed back there. Jernigan knew that the two men who had been posted behind the hotel had come to the street and run into the fire of that wild man.

Barron's rifle stopped firing, and Jernigan moved forward between the coach and the wall. Seeing the gunhand mounting his horse, he started running along the street.

"You, Barron!" he shouted, raging. "You lost *your* nerve, gunhand?"

Barron called back, "Another time, mustanger! Another time!"

He wheeled his horse about and started away, running the black.

Jernigan swore bitterly, a wild man himself now. Coming to a stop, he fired the three remaining loads in his revolver after the fleeing rider. He was simply giving vent to his rage, not expecting to bring the man down. Stace Barron disappeared into the darkness, gone from Rincon.

The shooting back along the street had stopped again, and Jernigan, punching the spent brass from his revolver and shoving in fresh loads, faced in that direction.

Matt Baylor was a hulking shape in front of the hotel.

With a wicked amusement, he called out, "Three of them down, and one on the run. But you didn't get the main one, mustanger. You let that ornery son get away. No matter. His luck will run out next time."

Jernigan watched him, saying nothing. He felt no exhilaration. At the moment the truth about Ed Jernigan was that he felt sickened by all the killing. He wished he were done with it.

"You did for six before tonight, bucko," Baylor went on, his amused voice loud and grating in the silence of the street. "With these three tonight, we've got Barron's crew cut down to half. By damn, mustanger; Crescent is ripe for plucking!"

The street had been empty of townspeople all this while, though almost every doorway and window had had one or more persons watching the gunfight. Now many men and some women ventured outside to gape at the dead men — and at the two men who had come through the shooting alive.

Jernigan walked away from those staring eyes. He walked past the jubilant Matt Baylor, ignoring his suggestion that they go have a drink. He also ignored the shouted command to halt that came from the town marshal, Mel Harper, when that worthy made his usual

128

tardy appearance. He walked out of the town, to where he had left his horse.

Riding slowly through the night, he continued to feel sickened by the killing he'd had to do. Before he had traveled far, he made up his mind to call it quits. His ranch wasn't worth so much bloodshed, wasn't so valuable that he should keep on laying his life on the line for it. He wasn't a running man, but simply one who'd had a bellyful of fighting.

He would return to his camp, pack his provisions and campgear on his spare horse, and leave this range forever.

XV

In the morning Jernigan was still of a mind to call it quits and move on to some other range. But he was the victim of inertia, and told himself: *Tomorrow . . . I'll ride on tomorrow.* When tomorrow came, he remained camped in the canyon.

At mid-afternoon Will Tolliver rode into the canyon at its east end. Jernigan watched him approach without interest. He was hunkered down by a boulder, puffiing on a cigarette.

Dismounting, Tolliver said, "Figured this canyon would be where you're holed up, Ed. It has the only water in this part of the hills."

"A little later, you wouldn't have found me here," Jernigan said. "I've decided to move on — to other parts."

"You feel you can't lick Crescent?"

"Not that. I've had too much fighting. I'm sick of killing."

"Hold on a little while longer, and the fighting will be done for you by Matt Baylor and the pack of fools he's talked into riding with him against that outfit."

Jernigan showed no interest. Nor did he feel any.

Tolliver leaned against a rock and began filling his pipe.

After puffing it alight, he went on, "Baylor has about fifteen of the ranchers throwing in with him to raid Crescent headquarters tomorrow night. He's also brought in a half dozen toughhands from outside the Basin — a mean looking lot. He plans to strike at midnight, hoping to catch everybody there asleep."

Jernigan showed some interest now, but not much. His only comment was, "In his way, Baylor is as bad as Stace Barron."

"At San Miguel last night he was doing a lot of bragging how he saved your hide at Rincon."

"He did that, to give the Devil his due," Jernigan said. "But only because he wanted some more of Barron's men killed."

"Well, I won't be riding with him tomorrow night," Tolliver said. "Nor will a lot of other Basin men. Even his partner, Jake Whittaker, backed out when he learned that Baylor plans to rob the Lelands."

"It shouldn't surprise anybody that Baylor plans to steal their cattle. He talked about it at the meeting."

"It's not the cattle he's after now, Ed. According to Jake, Baylor claims that the Lelands keep a lot of

130

money at the ranch. Thirty thousand dollars, he told Jake. Where he got that figure, I don't know."

"He has a friend out there who keeps him posted."

"One thing sure," Tolliver said, "he'll disappear with the money when the shooting is over. He won't share it, except maybe to pay off those toughhands he's imported."

"Like I told you," Jernigan said, "Matt Baylor is as bad in his way as Stace Barron is in his."

Tolliver nodded his agreement to that, and the two of them fell silent. The silence stretched on and on, and finally, his pipe smoked out, Tolliver seemed to feel he'd worn his welcome out. When he spoke of starting for home, Jernigan said nothing to dissuade him.

Once in the saddle, Tolliver said, "We've only to sit tight and wait for Baylor and his crowd to run Barron and what men he's got left out of the Basin. We'll be safe then. No sense in your moving on, Ed, when Crescent is about to go under."

Jernigan was noncommittal, saying merely, "You could be right."

An hour or so later as he bestirred himself to break camp, the words Will Tolliver had spoken really registered with him.

He felt a thrust of alarm, and with his mind's eye saw Matt Baylor and his crowd of toughhands and Crescent-hating ranchers making their midnight raid. All hell would break out, for Barron and his men — and even the four regular Crescent hands — would certainly put up a bitter fight. Shooting and bloodshed, the trapped men savage with desperation and the attackers gone berserk — with the Leland women caught between them.

Kitty Leland had helped bait him into the gun-trap at Rincon, but Jernigan no more wanted to see her come to harm than he did Margaret. He had to do something to keep that from happening.

While saddling the dun, he realized that the only thing he could do was to ride to Crescent and warn Margaret. That meant he would be risking his life again and probably have to do more killing, for Stace Barron was too much a hating man, too spiteful and vengeful, to end their feud even for his coming with such a warning.

The sun was lowering toward the far mountains when he rode from the canyon. It was just as well the day was going. He would slip up to Crescent's big ranchhouse under cover of darkness, have his talk with Margaret, and maybe get away without being spotted by Barron and his toughhands. Maybe.

Crescent lay southeast, and he headed in that direction at an easy lope — not hurrying, wanting nightfall to come. He now swung due south toward the buildings of the abandoned Carter ranch. Jeb Carter had been his nearest neighbor in this direction, and one of the first small ranchers to be driven out by the Barron crowd. Jernigan thought to stop at the place until dusk.

Drawing close to the buildings, which were replicas of his own, he saw that they were already showing signs of decay. Part of the corral fence was down, and one wall of the barn had begun to crumble.

132

Carter's water supply had been a well, and a wooden pail with an attached rope still stood on its stone wall. Jernigan dismounted and lowered the pail. A moment later he saw a rider coming along at a lope from the east — from the direction of the gap in the hills that led to his valley.

Thinking it was a Crescent hand, he reached for his rifle. The rider spotted him and swerved to swing wide of the Carter place. Almost too late he realized it was the person he wanted to see — Margaret Leland.

He ran out from the buildings, calling to her. She merely glanced over her shoulder and continued on her way. Then she looked again and this time pulled up. After a moment of staring at him uncertainly, she walked her mount toward him.

Going to meet her, Jernigan knew with certainty that if there was a woman with whom he could share his life it was this one. Only with her would his life be complete, and he be a whole man. He stood beside her horse, looking up at her without bothering to mask his feelings. And Margaret looked down at him in a frowning, wondering way, as though sensing that he had let her become all-important to him.

They were slow to speak, but finally Margaret said, "I was over to your ranch, Ed. I had Charley Faraday tell me how to get there. I'm so glad I didn't miss you entirely."

She let loose of the reins and held her left hand out to him, as though wanting him to touch her. As he took her hand, she swung down from the saddle and leaned against him briefly. Then, looking flustered, she caught up her horse's reins and led the animal toward the abandoned buildings.

Walking with her, Jernigan said, "Why were you looking for me, Margaret?"

"I learned last night — from Kitty — about the note Charley Faraday delivered to you. I wanted to tell you that I didn't write it."

"I knew you didn't — but too late."

She looked at him questioningly, and he told her how he had compared the writing in the note with her signature in the hotel register.

"Then I needn't have worried that you were blaming me — hating me."

"I couldn't hate you, Margaret."

They came into the weed-grown yard, stopped by the well, faced one another. Again Margaret appeared flustered, and yet met his gaze levelly.

After a long moment, she said, "Ed, after my husband was killed I was sure I could never care for another man. But you . . ." She smiled faintly. "And I hardly know you, really."

He reached for her, drew her to him. For a moment her lips were still as he kissed her; then suddenly they became warm and responsive — and briefly for Ed Jernigan there was no trouble in all the world. Only briefly. Margaret broke away from him, looking upset. She was frowning, biting her lower lip.

"This is no good, Ed," she said bleakly. "Nothing is right for us — can't be. You shouldn't be here on this range. Your life is in danger. And things are such a mess for me at Crescent that I —"

"Listen, Margaret, you've got to leave Crescent."

She shook her head. "Barron wouldn't let me go. He'd keep me there by force. He's vain enough to believe that I'll eventually marry him — and that way, through marriage, give him a firmer hold on the outfit. I'm as much his victim as Brad. I've learned from Kitty why Brad let him take over at Crescent. Brad is wanted under another name in San Francisco for bank robbery. Barron helped him get away, but now holds that over him. If Brad should turn against him, Barron would notify the law in San Francisco of his whereabouts.

"The only hope for either Brad or me is for somebody to kill Stace Barron. Despite what I told you the first time we talked, I do believe he killed my husband. I have only Brad's word that Barron was at ranch headquarters the night Steve was shot on the range — and I can't trust Brad. When I tried to hire you as a range detective, I did have it in mind that I might use you to get rid of that terrible man — heaven help me. But I succeeded only in placing you in danger, merely by being with you that morning."

She gripped Jernigan's arm. "Ed, go away — far away. Save yourself."

He shook his head to that, knowing now that he wouldn't run after all; then he told her about the raid Matt Baylor was planning.

"Go to Rincon, so you're safe," he ended up. "Stay at the hotel until this thing is over and done with. Go now, right from here."

He had gotten to her, he knew. She looked frightened.

135

But she said, "No, not now — not from here. I'll go back to Crescent, and leave from there in the morning. I'll take Kitty with me. I can't leave her there, with such a thing about to happen."

"Will Barron let you go, though?"

"To Rincon, yes. He'd stop me only if I tried to return to Kansas City."

She turned to her horse, mounted it.

"If you won't go away, Ed, then do keep out of harm's way — please."

He nodded to that, then watched her ride away. When she was far across the range, he swung onto his dun and rode back the way he had come. After traveling only a short distance, he turned in the direction of Will Tolliver's ranch. He had not treated Tolliver too well that afternoon at his camp in the canyon and now felt that he should make amends.

He let the dun find its own pace, and it loafed along. Dusk came, thickened into darkness. It was well after nightfall when he drew close to Tolliver's place, and then the sound of many ridden horses somewhere nearby in the darkness caused him to rein in and listen. The riders, a big bunch of them, were heading south, and seemed to have come from Tolliver's ranch.

Alarm was touched off in Jernigan, and he lifted his mount to a lope. He shouted for Tolliver as he rode into the yard.

"That you, Ed?" the man said from his doorway. "I thought that you —"

"Those riders," Jernigan broke in impatiently. "Who are they?"

136

"Matt Baylor and his gun-hung crowd," Tolliver said. "They stopped here to try to get me to ride along. They're on their way to raid Crescent one night early."

XVI

Now Ed Jernigan felt caught between the hammer and the anvil, and his confused thoughts kept him silent for so long that Will Tolliver came to him, alarmed, and said, "Ed, what ails you?"

"The women at Crescent," Jernigan said. "I'm thinking of what could happen to them — what is likely to happen to them."

"Yeah, there's that. I've been hating that outfit so hard I haven't given a thought to the chance of their coming to harm."

Jernigan hesitated a moment longer, then reined his horse about and started away.

Tolliver called, "Ed, what . . . ?"

"I'll see you later, Will."

Jernigan supposed he knew what he would do — because of Margaret. Because of Kitty Leland too. But he didn't like it. By warning the people at Crescent, he would be giving Stace Barron and his hardcases the chance to continue waging their range war — even be strengthening their position.

By the same token, he would be the cause of the Baylor crowd riding into a trap. He cared not at all that Matt Baylor and his imported toughhands might blunder into a murderous fire, but the ranchers in the bunch were a different matter. Jernigan knew he would have no peace of mind for a long time to come if some of them were killed because of his warning Crescent.

He felt that he would be damned if he did and damned if he didn't. So he might as well be damned for keeping the two young women from being endangered.

At the time he'd heard the twenty or more men in the Baylor crowd, they had been traveling at a lope — men of grim purpose in a hurry to reach their destination — to get about their ugly business. They had a long lead on him, and he was convinced they would attack as soon as they reached Crescent headquarters.

Jernigan lifted the dun to a run with a jab of his spurs. He had a full dozen miles to travel, and he had to reach Crescent ahead of the raiders. That would take some doing.

But he had easy going, for the Basin range was plains country, table-flat for the most part, and there was a moon to light the way for him.

He had covered about half the distance to Crescent when he saw the big bunch of horsemen almost directly ahead. He held his mount in now, reined it to a stop, to let it blow for a while. He knew he would reach his destination in time.

Matt Baylor and his followers were at the moment traveling at only a brisk walk. Getting down from the saddle, he caught the sound of voices — carried to him by a stiff breeze. The loud talk suggested drunkenness. He guessed that some of the bunch had brought bottles along and were pulling at them while on the way. Some of those men, especially some of the ranchers, would need whiskey courage for such an undertaking.

Mounting again, Jernigan rode at an easy lope and bore to the east to bypass the riders ahead. He passed within sight and sound of them, and heard a lusty voice — Matt Baylor's he guessed — call out.

"You there, hombre! Pull up! Pull up, I say!"

Jernigan ignored that and, holding his horse to its steady lope, swung back on a southwestward course to put himself ahead of the other riders. Looking back, he saw a half dozen or more of them trying to overtake him — or to get within bullet range of him. They would be, he supposed, afraid he was a Crescent hand riding to alert the people at the ranch headquarters.

Sourly amused, he thought: *Well, they're sure half right*.

The last couple of miles it was a race between him and three of the others. Those three, evidently better mounted than the rest of the bunch, tried their best to shorten his lead. But his dun, which had originally been a mustang, still ran strongly, and finally he topped a rise and saw the dark shapes of Crescent's buildings directly ahead.

Riding toward them, he drew his revolver and fired three shots into the air. The blasts of the Colt's .45 shattered the night quiet like claps of thunder. And should, he thought, wake even the soundest sleepers in both bunkhouse and ranchhouse. He rode on past the buildings, no longer pursued by the Baylor men. The three in the lead had reined in atop the rise and in a moment were joined by several other riders.

Facing in their direction, Jernigan cupped his hands to his mouth and shouted, "You, Matt Baylor . . . You hear me, Baylor? This is Ed Jernigan!"

He heard the man curse him bitterly.

"Crescent's warned," he yelled. "You haven't a chance taking this place. Turn back with your men before the lot of you get shot to pieces!"

He saw lamplight bloom against the bunkhouse windows, and thought: *Some damn fool needs a light to pull on his pants.* To Matt Baylor the light was a beacon — a red cloth waved at a surly bull. Again, as in Rincon that other night, Baylor turned into a wild man.

He shouted, "Come on, come on!" and led the half dozen men with him on the rise in a charge toward the buildings. More of his bunch appeared over there, and they raced after the first lot. He kept shouting, "Come on, come on!"

The raiders surged into the ranchyard, milled about there in wild confusion — shouting and shooting. The light in the bunkhouse went out, and now guns in that building and in the ranchhouse added their racket to the mounting din. The spurts of powderflame lit the yard like devilish fireworks.

Sitting his horse beyond the buildings, Jernigan took in the sights and sounds of this nightmare with a vast disgust for the senselessness of it all. He heard hit men cry out now, and he saw riderless horses running loose. The curses of frightened men reached him, and soon he watched some of the raiders take flight. The first who fled crested the rise yonder and disappeared.

140

Others followed in their wake, and the shooting diminished in intensity and then ceased.

One last man fled the yard, leaving behind a half dozen sprawled figures. He fled on foot, and a downed horse showed that he'd had his mount shot from under him. He was cursing loudly, bitterly, and Jernigan knew by his voice that he was Matt Baylor.

Baylor tried to catch up a riderless horse, the mount of one of the men lying dead or wounded. The horse eluded him and ran in Jernigan's direction with empty stirrups flapping. Baylor chased after it, still cursing, and then saw the mustanger and came to an abrupt halt.

Jernigan had lingered longer than was necessary, and now wondered if this was why: because he felt this man should have a chance to even matters with him. He swung down from the saddle with his rifle and stood braced for Baylor's play.

Matt Baylor's fury was suddenly spent, leaving him quite calm. He spoke in a conversational tone, even though behind each word lay the expected hatred and venom.

"This is twice you've tripped me up, mustanger," he said. "But you won't again — ever. I owe you this — for both Chuck and myself."

He had his gun in his hand, and he brought it up and fired far faster than Jernigan had expected. The mustanger was hit, and knew he was badly hit. He staggered under the impact of the slug that tore into him, but with an effort overcame the shock and recovered his balance sufficiently to drive a shot at

141

Baylor. The last thing he saw before his vision blurred was that his slug had found its mark and Baylor was going down.

Then he, too, was falling. He hit the ground jarringly, but the instinct to survive remained with him. Just as an injured animal might try to crawl away from its hurt, Jernigan tried to drag himself away from his terrible pain.

And from the vengeance of Stace Barron as well.

XVII

By instinct rather than conscious thought, Jernigan crawled toward his horse. He saw the dun dimly, through a dark-red mist lying behind his eyes, and it seemed a far way off. But he got close enough to reach out a hand and grope for the left stirrup.

The dun and he had been one and the same during all these days and nights of trouble, but now it shied away from him. Thus thwarted, he dropped his reaching hand and for a moment lay helpless.

He realized in a fuzzy way that the horse was made skittish by this strange thing that crawled on the ground.

"Easy, boy . . . Easy. It's me, and I'm not going to hurt you."

His voice was weak, and sounded odd to his own ears. But the dun must have recognized it, and been reassured. It now stood firm, and he got his hold on the stirrup. Gritting his teeth against knife-sharp thrusts of pain in his left side, he hauled himself up — hand over hand — until he gained his feet and had a grip on the saddle horn. He endured more pain when taking hold of the trailing reins. He next attempted to haul himself to the saddle, and on the second try made it.

As usual, the dun was in motion before he was seated and had found the right stirrup — and he was nearly toppled from its back. He saved himself by clutching its mane.

Behind him he heard a feeble but hating voice cursing him, and knew that Matt Baylor, like himself, clung to life though badly wounded.

He heard, too, from farther away, other voices — excited voices of the Crescent people now venturing outside bunkhouse and ranchhouse. Shortly the only sound for him was the steady clop-clopping of the dun's hooves as the animal carried him away from everything but his pain.

He let the horse have its head, for he wasn't clear-minded enough to guide it. He could only hope that it would take him back to his camp in the canyon. Again instinct alone, not reasoning power, told him he must get there to be safe.

The dun moved along steadily, at a brisk walk, for what seemed to Jernigan an eternity. At times he was barely conscious, and on occasion caught himself slumping far forward — on the verge of falling from the saddle. Pain was always with him, and in his lucid moments he realized that his blood — and his strength — kept flowing from his wound.

Finally his will alone could no longer sustain him. He let himself go and was engulfed by black nothingness. For an instant he had the sensation of falling . . . knew he was spilling from the saddle — and did not care.

Regaining his senses after a time, he found himself sprawled on his stomach with his face pressed against the ground. He managed to turn onto his back, and lay staring up at the star-studded sky. He didn't know where he was, and didn't wonder about it for long. He was content just to remain still, in an unthinking state. His left side had become numb. He was tired to the core of himself, and knew that meant his strength was mostly gone.

Finally he slept.

And awoke to full daylight, with the sun already high.

He was immediately aware of a craving for water, of a great thirst that threatened to become a torment. He struggled to rise, failed. The most he could do was to prop himself up briefly on his elbows. A quick glance around, before he fell back, showed him that the dun had tried to take him not to his camp but home. He was lying midway through the gap in the hills, a short half-mile from his buildings.

The horse was gone, no doubt having continued into the valley, despite its trailing reins, in search of water and grass.

Water . . . Jernigan was famished for water.

He was lying in the full glare of the sun, and by slow stages he managed to drag himself into the scant shade of some of the boulders with which the narrow pass was strewn.

I'll rest a little while, he told himself, *then go down there*.

He tried without success to convince himself that he would eventually be able to make it down to the creek — and that after drinking his full he would be all right.

His great pain had not returned but a dull, throbbing ache afflicted his left side from shoulder to hip. He became aware that his wound had stopped bleeding, but too late . . . far too late to have kept his strength from ebbing.

Time passed. How much, he did not know. The sun climbed higher, stealing his shade. He thought of trying to move out, to go to the creek, but knew the effort required was beyond him. He let himself think that this was the end of the trail for him, and accepted it fatalistically. Looking back with his mind's eye, he saw that it had been a rough trail indeed. He'd done his share of hard work and occasionally he'd had a little fun. But he hadn't left much of a mark along the way, and he wouldn't be leaving anything of himself behind. There wasn't even anyone who would cherish his memory.

Would Margaret, maybe — a little while?

He thought of her with fondness, and with the regret that he had not been able to get rid of Stace Barron for her.

His bleak reverie was interrupted by the clatter of shod hooves striking rocky ground, and when he forced himself up on his elbows he saw a rider coming through the pass . . . coming slowly, like a tracker.

Stace Barron.

Jernigan felt no surprise. This confrontation had been inevitable, for Barron had finally become satisfied that he had the edge. He must have learned from Matt Baylor that it had been he, Ed Jernigan, who had warned Crescent of its danger — and who had wounded him. Baylor would have told it that he had put a bullet in the mustanger, and so Barron, having his edge, had set out to track his enemy down.

Looking up from the hoof marks he followed, the gunhand saw Jernigan lying there ahead. He immediately reined in his black horse and jerked his rifle from its boot. Then he realized that the mustanger lay there helpless, not in ambush.

Jernigan let himself sink down, unable to bear the strain of keeping his upper body raised.

Barron rode a few yards closer, and called out, "I could put a bullet into you, mustanger, but that" — his voice held a wicked amusement — "would put you out of your misery — and you'd welcome it. I'd rather you die slow — and hard."

He booted his rifle, took a cheroot from his shirt pocket.

Jernigan, his head turned in an awkward way that made his neck ache, watched the gunhand strike a match and puff the cheroot alight.

"Of course, if you'd beg me to finish you off . . ." Barron pretended to consider that, then shook his head. "No, not even then — because of your rolling me in that dirt that day. And because of the woman, Jernigan. You warned us last night only because of her. I savvy that. But I've staked a claim to her, and because you tried to jump it, you'll have to be a long, hard time dying."

Jernigan said nothing. He was trying to muster enough strength to make one desperate play. His will to live had firmed up since the gunhand's arrival. That black horse ... it might be the means by which he could save his life.

Barron said, "I'm carrying water, mustanger." He lifted a canteen from his saddle horn, swung it by its strap, then hurled it in Jernigan's direction. It fell midway between them. "Wounded men always crave water" he taunted. "So help yourself to it."

Jernigan found the strength somewhere. He heaved over onto his stomach and drew his gun, coming close to crying out with the pain the effort caused him. The long-barreled Colt had grown too heavy for him, but by using both hands he was able to level it and thumb back its hammer.

Barron reacted the instant the mustanger began his difficult play. He spat out his cheroot, wheeled his horse about, and started away. His back was target enough, but when Jernigan got off his shot, his hands were too shaky with weakness. The slug went wide of its mark.

Barron dismounted out of reach of the handgun, and shouted, "So you can still bite, eh? A lot of good it will do you!"

Jernigan again drew on his feeble strength and crawled in among a cluster of rocks. He opened the loading gate of his revolver, ejected the brass of a fired cartridge and with shaky fingers fed in a fresh load from his belt. He repeated this action until he had the weapon fully loaded. He was convinced that in the end Barron would find no satisfaction in leaving him to die but would be driven to trying to kill him with his own hand. And now that he was behind adequate cover, the gunhand would have to come closer to get a clear shot at him. If he could only steady his hands, he would have a chance at that black horse.

Barron moved beneath an overhang of rock at the side of the cut, where he was in the shade. He hunkered down and lit another cheroot, seemingly still resolved to let Jernigan die slowly. Now another rider came into the gap. It was Margaret Leland, Jernigan saw. Barron must have known she was following him, for he did not so much as glance at her.

She reined in beside Barron's black horse and, ignoring the gunhand, kept looking about until she saw Jernigan in the rocks.

Kneeing her mount into motion, she rode closer and then stopped midway between the two men.

"Ed, are you badly hurt?"

"Bad enough," he said, his voice coming from his parched throat and mouth as a croak. "I can't do any moving about — to get at him."

Margaret now saw the canteen and rode to where it lay. She dismounted, evidently intending to pick it up and take it to Jernigan. Before she reached it, Barron's rifle cracked and the canteen was kicked a little distance from its resting place. Water leaked from the holes the slug left.

148

At the shot Margaret had stopped short. Now she went on without looking to see if Barron intended to fire again. Jernigan feared that the man would, and tried to call to her to get back. But Barron didn't endanger her. Margaret picked up the bullet-drilled canteen and held her hands against the holes to stem the leakage of water.

As on the morning in Rincon, the gunhand lost his icy control because of her. He shouted, raging, "No, you don't! I won't have it, by damn!"

He came running to intercept her.

Jernigan managed to get out a hoarse shout. "Margaret, drop down!"

She had the presence of mind to obey instantly. By flattening herself to the ground, she gave him a clear line of fire. And as the enraged man came within reach of his gun, Jernigan drove a shot at him.

Barron stopped running, not hit but alerted to his danger. By the time Jernigan got his revolver cocked and aimed again, the gunhand was firing into the rocks. Barron had only a small target, for little of the mustanger was exposed. He was also handicapped by his lack of self-control. He got off three fast shots before Jernigan was able to fire again. The slugs struck the rocks about the mustanger, one screaming as it ricocheted. This time Jerigan's aim was good. His bullet caught Barron in the chest. As the gunhand staggered, Jernigan fired into him again. Barron now collapsed, and was dead by the time he hit the ground.

Jernigan had used up the last remnant of his strength. He let his gun fall, and dropped his arms and head to the earth.

Margaret came into the rocks to him.

"Ed, try to raise your head — please!"

He tried and succeeded, and greedily drank the water she let trickle from one of the holes in the canteen. She allowed him only a small ration, denied him more for a moment. He could have drunk a well dry, and in a short time, with small, spaced gulps, he did empty the canteen.

"I'll need more," he told Margaret. "Ride down to the creek at my ranch."

She went, and returned shortly with the canteen filled. She had plugged the bullet holes with pieces of cloth torn from her blouse and small bits of wood she'd managed to find. She let him drink his fill now, and afterward helped him crawl from the rocks. He lay on his back, more comfortable now but still feeling near the end of his rope.

He looked at her wonderingly as she knelt beside him, and asked, "You knew he was coming after me?"

She nodded. "He talked with the man you shot."

"Matt Baylor."

"Yes. He was dying, but managed to say that he had wounded you. At daylight Barron set out to find you, and I followed him."

"And saved my life."

"I'm not so sure I have saved your life, Ed," Margaret said, troubled. "You look so — so terrible. I must get you to the doctor — somehow."

150

"Will Tolliver has a wagon," Jernigan said. "He'll haul me to Rincon. His place is north of here . . ."

He told her how to find Tolliver's ranch, and Margaret immediately set out for there.

And Ed Jernigan would have bet, and given odds, that he would pull through.

Late one morning, two weeks later, Jernigan once more rode up to Crescent Ranch's fine headquarters. He was feeling fit again, except for a lingering soreness at his left side, and looking his normal self too. He was freshly barbered and wearing new clothes, from hat to boots, as was only fitting for a man calling on his young lady.

Gruff, short-tempered Dr. Harvey had patched him up expertly. The Widow Gomez had taken him in and given him the same good care she had lavished on Miguel Rojas.

Margaret had come to see him several times, and now he was visiting Crescent on her invitation. She had told him that she was alone here now, except for the four regular ranchhands whom Barron hadn't gotten rid of when taking over as boss of the outfit. With the gunhand dead, the surviving members of his hardcased crew had departed for other climes. So had Brad Leland, taking along his wife, Kitty, and her father, Ben Hazlitt.

"Brad also took the ranch's money," Margaret had told Jernigan. "More than thirty thousand dollars. But it was a cheap enough price to be rid of him."

No signs of the gun battle that had taken place here remained, and for Jernigan the whole of the trouble was

151

a dimming memory. It was that for the entire Rincon Basin, for Margaret certainly would not wage a range war against her neighbors.

She appeared as he reined in before the ranchhouse, and today he saw her in a different role. She was wearing a plain green gingham dress with an apron over it. She wiped her hands on the apron while coming to him. She had a smudge of flour on her left cheek. Her face was flushed from bending over a hot cookstove. A wisp of her red-brown hair dangled over her forehead. He decided that he liked her this way best of all.

"You told me to stop by when I was able," he said, removing his brand-new hat. Then, with his old devil-may-care grin: "I guess I'm as able as I need to be."

Margaret didn't appear amused. She said, almost curtly, "I've dinner about ready. Put up your horse and come in."

He nodded, swung down from the saddle, started to lead his dun toward the corral, then looked at her again.

"You're pretty sober today. Is something wrong?"

"Of course something is wrong," Margaret said. "I have this outfit to run, and it's too much for a woman. When I think of all that must be seen to, I want to pack up and leave."

"What you need is a man about the place, the kind of man who could take charge and let you tend to your housekeeping."

"Now where would I find a man I could trust?"

"Well, ma'am, I reckon I'm about the most trustworthy hombre around. I'm too mule-contrary to be otherwise."

"Are you proposing to me, Ed Jernigan?"

He saw now that her eyes held a mischievous glint, that she wasn't in as sober a mood as she appeared.

Grinning, he said, "No, ma'am, I was just offering to take on the job of bossing this outfit — to help you out. But if a man has to marry you to get the job . . . well, I reckon I could find it in me to pop the question."

Margaret smiled in the happy way of a woman given proof that she was wanted by the man of her choice. "We'll consider it done," she said. "That you've proposed and I've said 'yes.' Now get along and put up your horse."

Jernigan said, "Yes, ma'am. I'll be along in no time at all."

Leading his dun to the corral, he saw how the future would be for him. He would boss the Crescent outfit and Margaret would boss him. But that didn't seem a bad prospect at all. In fact, he had a notion it would be far better than mustanging back in the Brenoso Badlands.